D1637381

I ESCAPED THE WORLD'S DEADLIEST SHARK ATTACK

THE SINKING OF THE USS INDIANAPOLIS, WW2

ELLIE CROWE

SCOTT PETERS

PROPERTY OF
BEEBE LIBRARY
345 MAIN STREET
WAKEFIELD, MA

BDB

BEST DAY BOOKS
FOR YOUNG READERS

FEB - - 2021

If you purchased this book without a cover, you should be aware this is stolen property. It was reported as "stripped and destroyed" to the publisher, and neither the author nor the publisher has received any payment for this "stripped book."

I Escaped The World's Deadliest Shark Attack (I Escaped Book Three)

Copyright © 2019 by Ellie Crowe and Scott Peters

All rights reserved.

No part of this book may be reproduced in any form or by any electronic or mechanical means, including information storage and retrieval systems, without written permission from the author, except for the use of brief quotations in a book review.

Library of Congress Control Number: 2019914362

ISBN: 978-1-951019-04-4 (Hardcover)

ISBN: 978-1-951019-07-5 (Paperback)

While inspired by real events, this is a work of fiction and does not claim to be historically accurate or portray factual events or relationships. References to historical events, real persons, business establishments and real places are used fictitiously and may not be factually accurate, but rather fictionalized by the author.

Photos: Great White by Olga Ernst CC by SA 4.0, *Sun Over Ocean* by kein CC by SA 2.0, *Shark* by Bernard-Dupont CC by SA 2.0

Cover design by Susan Wyshynski

Best Day Books For Young Readers

ISOS - - 837

For Raine Prsa.
Thanks for encouraging us to write about these brave sailors.

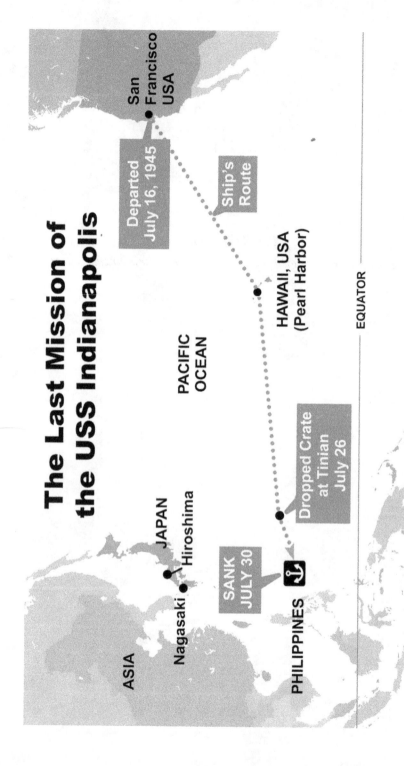

The Last Mission of the USS Indianapolis

CHAPTER 1

MONDAY JULY 30, 1945
THE PHILIPPINE SEA
00:30 HOURS

THE USS INDIANAPOLIS—THE invincible warship, the flagship of the United States Navy—was split in two, on fire, and sinking fast. Leaping from the deck, Josh hit the water with a stinging belly flop. Down he spiraled, down, down into the pitch-dark ocean. Swirling blackness surrounded him. Mind spinning, heart racing, he somersaulted, trying to work out which way was up.

Was that the moon shining through the sea? He kicked furiously, his legs struggling against the leaden weight of his boots. The kapok life vest, already waterlogged when he put it on, could barely do its job.

Come on, come on! Almost there!

Flaying wildly, he broke into the open air, gasping in long heaving breaths.

To his horror, a nasty sight waited—the sinking warship's propellers churning in huge, powerful strokes, ready to grind him to pieces. The massive metal blades could cut clean through an army of men. Frantic, he threw himself backward.

"She'll suck us under," a voice screamed. "Swim! Swim!"

Above, sailors still swarmed the tilting vessel, teeming like ants on a stick. How could this be happening? Moments ago, they'd all been high and dry. Now, he was swimming with no land in sight for hundreds of miles.

The pull of the dying ship sucked him closer. Terrified but refusing to give in, Josh clawed at the water. His dungarees hamstrung his legs and his boots felt like anvils. Every stroke was a fight.

He was out of his element in this surging sea. Totally out of it. He was sixteen, a baseball player from San Antonio, Texas. A good athlete. But the ocean wasn't his world. He was no Olympic swimmer—why on earth had he ever joined the Navy?

The USS Indianapolis groaned and shrieked. Then, in a terrible death plunge, the massive warship disappeared carrying the men still aboard into the dark depths.

Cascades of water crashed over Josh's head, pulling at his limbs.

I'm being sucked down.

His mind reeled, fear flooded his body as he again found himself flailing beneath the surface. His ears exploded. His eyeballs popped.

All he could hear was the ship, like a dying monster, moaning way down below. He could still see the lights from raging flames glowing through the portholes. They blazed in the lonely darkness as the mighty boat sank toward its watery grave. And he was going with it. Spiraling down. Down.

He couldn't hold his breath much longer. Any moment, his lungs would give up and he'd gulp in water. That, he knew, would be the end of him. He'd never see home, never see his mom and kid brother Sammy, never get to say goodbye.

He was so deep he could no longer see any light. He kicked, but which way was up? What if he was kicking down further?

His life vest still had some strength in it for it tugged at him, pulling his shoulders away from his legs. Suddenly, like a miracle, the boat lost its powerful drag. Released, Josh shot upward. For good measure, he kicked with all he had left. Like a cork, he exploded to the surface, vomiting fuel oil and saltwater.

He coughed and coughed, sucked in air until his lungs stopped aching and he could see straight again.

Thank God he'd pulled on a life vest. Without it, he'd probably still be down there.

The full moon appeared from behind the clouds. Bright yellow light slashed across the rough swells. Ahead of him, something moved.

He stayed motionless as the shape disappeared behind a wave. The ocean heaved, and it reappeared.

It was a person. Another sailor. What a relief.

"Hey!" Josh shouted. "Wait for me!"

Kicking and splashing, he swam toward the man.

"Hey!" Josh called again. Then stopped swimming.

The man was staring at him.

With zombie eyes.

The top half of the man's body, still wearing a life vest, rose high into the air. Then crashed back down into the water. And disappeared. Like something had pulled him under. Blinking, treading furiously, Josh stared. What the heck? He wiped engine oil from his stinging eyes and tried to focus.

Then the man's life jacket popped up.

Empty.

Suddenly Josh saw them—the dark, white-tipped fins—slicing their way through the ocean. Slowly. Smoothly. Surely. Beginning to circle.

Deep in his gut, he knew what they were.

Sharks.

He swallowed hard. Pictured his feet dangling beneath him in the blackness. Drew his legs in tight. There was nothing to scramble on top of. No way to climb clear.

His fists were his only weapons.

And he was surrounded by hundreds of man-eating sharks.

CHAPTER 2

```
THIRTY MINUTES EARLIER
MONDAY JULY 30, 1945
THE PHILIPPINE SEA
00:00 HOURS
```

MIDNIGHT. Joshua Layton, sixteen years old, had finished his watch on the USS Indianapolis. Whistling, he made his way along the winding corridors.

The mighty warship was heading from San Francisco to the port of Leyte in the Philippines, through choppy seas and long rolling swells. The ship shook with the violence of the spinning propellers, the roar of the powerful engines.

Must be pushing the engines to the max, Josh thought. Wherever we're going, someone in charge wants to get there fast. Well, that's fine with me.

He knew his way around the warship now. Mostly, anyway. The USS Indianapolis was huge, the length of two football fields. After two weeks at sea, he almost felt at home.

They'd only made one stop, a brief one at the United States Army Air Force Base on the island of Tinian in Guam. The crew had unloaded a mysterious canister and crate before heading back out to sea. As to what that cargo contained, no one had any clue. Airplane parts? A new, high tech weapon? Food supplies? He'd probably never find out.

The USS Indianapolis Underway

Whatever the case, it was good to be part of the action, to be one of the men fighting the Japanese, the enemy who'd killed his dad.

Although World War II raged in Europe and in the Pacific, on the Indy all was calm and under control. And Josh was hungry. He lifted his arm and sniffed his blue shirt. Phew, he stank. I should have a shower, he thought, but I'm starved. They work you hard in the Navy!

Luckily he knew just where to get something good to eat. Still whistling, he snuck into the officer's wardroom—the officers always had the best food. He checked out the leftovers. The egg and mayo sandwiches looked good. He grabbed two, wrapped them in waxed sandwich paper, and slipped them into the top pocket of his blue dungarees.

Quickly he looked around the table, checking for leftover dessert. Pete, also wearing his blue shirt and blue dungarees, was digging into a chocolate cake.

Pete grinned at Josh. "Cake's good."

Josh laughed. "The officers sure have great desserts!" He already knew the chocolate cake with the super-gooey chocolate icing was the best. And he knew they wouldn't mind if he took a thin slice or two. The officers on the USS Indianapolis were good guys. Pete's cousin was a lieutenant. He'd told them the leftovers in the officers' wardroom were up for grabs after midnight.

Josh had met Pete two weeks ago when they'd boarded the warship in San Francisco. Josh was fresh from boot camp. He'd been glad to see so many other sailors were young, too. Not as young as he was, for Josh had lied to the recruiting officer—the Navy didn't accept sixteen-year-olds. You had to be eighteen to enlist, or seventeen if you had your parents' permission. But a lot of the other guys looked barely older than him. And there were so many guys. More than a thousand!

Pete swallowed a mouthful of cake. Icing stuck to his chin. "I just heard something weird," he said. "My cousin Mike, he's a lieutenant, he says we're on a secret mission."

Josh looked up with interest. "Yeah?"

"Remember that big crate and canister the Marines loaded before we left San Francisco?" Pete said. "The ones we offloaded in Tinian Island?"

Josh nodded. Funny, he'd just been thinking about that. "Yeah. What's in them?"

"He doesn't know. Something important, though.

Remember all that top brass on the wharf and those planes flying protective formations overhead?"

"Yeah. And all those Marines with guns!"

"Exactly. Mike was one of those armed Marines. He says it's real important stuff," Pete said. "So important, no one's allowed to know what was inside, only maybe Captain McVay. And President Truman. It's all top secret."

"Okay!" Josh tried to look cool. Wow. A secret mission! That must be why they'd called up the crew so fast. He wished he was one of the Marines with the lethal-looking guns. Maybe in the Philippines, he'd be accepted for gunnery training. Then he could be one of the gun crew.

"You going to start gunnery training?" he asked Pete.

Pete laughed. The guy's red-hair and freckles reminded him of his kid brother, Sammy. "I wish. Joe says I won't be doing anything exciting soon. He says we're all too *green*, and the Navy's going to train us at Leyte. In the Philippines. Until we get there, he says I'll be scrubbing decks." He grimaced

"I hope we invade Japan soon!" Josh said. This was what he wanted to do. This was why he enlisted in the Navy. Why he lied and gave his age as seventeen. Why he'd forged his mom's signature on the Parental Consent Form.

The Japanese killed his dad when they bombed Pearl Harbor, Hawaii. That was over three years ago now: December 7th, 1941, two and a half weeks before the worst Christmas of his life. He, Mom, and Sammy were shattered, lost without him. The Japanese had broken his family. The sooner he could fight the enemy, the better. They had to be stopped. He owed it to his father, the best person in the world he'd ever known.

Josh swallowed hard, wiped the sweat from his forehead. Ran his fingers over his dark curly hair, spiky in his new Navy buzz-cut. July in the Pacific was hot. "I'm heading to the forward turret," he said. "Got permission to sleep up there tonight."

"Good for you," Pete said. "It's an oven down in the bunkroom."

Josh grabbed a slice of chocolate cake, wrapped it in sandwich paper, too, and filled his canteen with water. He was glad to be sleeping out on deck. He'd picnic. Write a letter to Mom and Sammy. Tell them how much he missed them. Tell them he was fine, that life on board was great.

First, though, he needed to pay a visit to the head. Sort of a weird name for the toilet, but that was the Navy for you. He'd had to learn a lot of odd names for all sorts of things.

Agile as a monkey, he climbed a steel ladder to the forecastle deck.

He hopped inside the head, shut the door, and unbuckled his dungarees.

The first torpedo struck.

CHAPTER 3

MONDAY JULY 30, 1945
THE PHILIPPINE SEA
00:15 HOURS

THE EXPLOSION FLUNG Josh sideways in the tiny cubicle. His head slammed into the basin. He crashed to the floor, seeing stars. What the heck! What was that? Ears ringing, he struggled to his feet.

The second explosion knocked him to his knees.

He staggered and shoved open the door.

Someone screamed, "Look out!"

A wall of flames shot down the corridor, burning his face. He yelled and jumped back.

Then came the third explosion.

The massive warship lurched to starboard. Thick black smoke poured down the hall, making him choke and cough.

What the heck? I've got to get outta here!

Heart pounding, eyes wide in disbelief, he saw flames

blazing in both directions. If he ran through this, he'd be torched.

But if he stayed . . . Flipping out, he turned the seawater tap on full blast and splashed seawater all over his body, soaking his denim shirt and dungarees. Wrapping a wet towel around his head, he raced down the corridor, leaping through the heat and flickering flames.

He kept going, scrambling up a metal ladder. With relief, he saw the night sky above. He'd made it out. But the place was a madhouse.

Half-naked sailors, pulled from their beds, charged around deck. Who was in charge?

A man's high-pitched scream rang out, "Help! Help me!"

Josh raced to the railing and peered over. Stunned, he saw that the bow—the front end of the warship—was gone. Completely gone! Swallowed up by the waves. The Indy had been split in two. Yet somehow the massive warship's back end still plowed ahead through the ocean. Insane. This thing must be taking on thousands of gallons of water. Fast. Scooping it straight into the decks below.

With a wrenching snap, the steel-plated deck cracked open beneath his feet. Flames and smoke poured through as he jumped sideways. A pillar of fire shot from the ship's heart into the sky. The fuel tanks must have copped it, were pouring fuel on the blaze. It lit up the whole world in gruesome fiery reds and blacks. Waves of heat wobbled in the air. What remained of the Indy was burning fast.

Two sailors struggled to work a fire hose then flung it down.

"No water pressure," a red-faced man shouted.

Josh had no idea where to go, but the cracks underfoot were widening. He raced across the burning deck, slipped in what looked like blood, nearly lost his balance. Around him, injured sailors and officers yelled and screamed. Metallic, high-pitched sounds tore through the night—sounds you prayed you'd never hear on a ship: metal ripping, electrical cords sparking. Thick smoke mushroomed from the forward deck.

"What's going on?" someone roared "Do we abandon ship?"

Wildly, Josh wondered when someone would take control of this madness. Were they supposed to abandon ship? Captain McVay hadn't given the command.

He pictured the black ocean roiling below, and his stomach clenched. It was safer on the Indy. The warship had survived battles and even direct hits before. A ship this size wouldn't just sink. They'd seal bulkheads, find a way to keep the water out.

"We're goners," a young sailor screamed.

"Put on a life vest," an older man replied. "We ain't gone yet, are we?"

Life vests. Mine's in the bunkroom! I need another one. Fast.

Josh knew where the emergency buoyancy devices were kept. He raced to join two sailors cutting a net holding bundles of kapok life vest, pulling his jackknife from his calf holster as he ran.

With relief, he spotted the tall figure of Lieutenant Commander Moore.

"She's taking on too much water," Moore shouted. "We have to stop the flooding." He turned to an officer. "Where's the Captain?"

"I don't know. Communications are down, Sir," the officer replied.

"Why haven't they stopped the engines?" Moore demanded.

"We don't know, we can't reach them on the radio."

Lieutenant Commander Moore turned to Josh. "Sailor!" he barked. "Get down to that engine room. Tell Chief Engineer Redmayne his orders are to stop the engines and close the watertight doors. Immediately."

Who? Me?

No way did Josh want to go back down! The engine room was below the waterline, deep in the ship's bowels. The absolute worst place to be if the ship sank. He'd be trapped. There'd be no way out.

"Yes, Sir," he said, almost choking on the words.

CHAPTER 4

MONDAY JULY 30, 1945
THE PHILIPPINE SEA
00:17 HOURS

HANDS SIZZLING on the metal ladder rungs, Josh descended into the billowing smoke. Rung by rung. It felt like suicide. It probably was. Adrenaline flooded his body. His mind urged him to flee. He wanted to flee. His legs shook. *Run! Get out of here. Fast!*

He forced himself to keep climbing down.

Emergency lights cast eerie shadows everywhere. Panicked men pushed past, going the other way. The way he wanted to go. Shouting at him and cursing.

"Move over!"

"Get outta here!"

"Idiot! What are you doing? You're going the wrong way!"

Josh longed to join them. He'd deliver the message, then he'd get out.

Coughing, choking, he groped his way deeper until he finally reached the engine room. As he stepped inside, an officer pushed past. Josh caught the officer's arm. "Sir, I've got a message for Chief Engineer Redmayne," he stammered. "Captain's orders are to stop the engines."

"The Chief isn't here," the officer said, his face dripping with sweat. "Communications are down. We've had no such orders. The Chief has gone to find the Captain."

"Sir, orders from the bridge are to stop the engines," Josh said. "Immediately."

The officer looked confused. "Sailor, I have no authority to do that. There's only one engine left anyway. If we stop moving, we'll be a better target for the Japs."

Sparks flew from the ventilator ducts, showering him and the men. The ship tilted and let out a sickening screech.

A sailor bellowed, "Clear out! Everyone. Go. GO!"

"Don your life vests!" someone shouted.

This was crazy. Why hadn't he grabbed a life vest when he had the chance? He'd have to sprint to his bunkroom, grab his life vest, and get back on deck.

The corridor teetered at an angle as he raced, slip-sliding. At his sleeping room door, he reeled back. The once quiet refuge was a disaster zone. Bunk racks had collapsed. Smashed bed frames littered the floor. Sailors, thrown from their bunks, writhed under the wreckage.

"Help me. Help!" a man screamed. "I'm stuck!"

"Men, give me a hand," came the deep voice of Marine Private First Class McCoy.

Josh raced to join McCoy. Furiously, they began digging victims out from under the fallen lockers and rubble.

An open hatch led to an upper corridor.

Under it, a chain of uninjured men pushed the wounded

up the ladder. Everywhere, faces were tense with fear. Everyone worked as fast as possible, all waiting for their chance to get up the ladder and out the hatch, the only way out.

The ship tilted sharply. Josh lost his footing and fell, landing hard on a trapped sailor. The guy, who looked no older than Josh, cried out in pain.

"I'm sorry. I'm sorry!" Josh stammered.

How could this even be happening? This was insane!

"Get me out," the sailor begged, his face scrunched in agony. "My arm, it's stuck."

Josh nodded, unsure if he could lift the metal cabinet trapping the guy against the floor. "Hold on." Gritting his teeth, Josh braced against it and pushed hard. A second later, he freed the sailor. Eyes unfocused in pain, the guy staggered to his feet.

From above, a voice rang out. "Sorry, men. We're dogging the hatch."

Dogging the hatch? Did that mean . . .

"No!" Josh screamed. "No, wait!"

He couldn't believe his ears. They were closing the hatch? With all of them still below? He and these men would be trapped! If the ship sank, they'd die.

"Hold on, wait," he shouted. "We'll be buried alive!"

With a sickening thud, the hatch slammed shut.

CHAPTER 5

MONDAY JULY 30, 1945
THE PHILIPPINE SEA
00:19 HOURS

IN A REMOTE, reasoning section of his brain, Josh understood what was happening. The hatches had to be closed to stop the ship from sinking. The USS Indianapolis had to be made watertight. He and these injured men would be sacrificed to save the others. They'd be sacrificed to save the ship.

That knowledge didn't make it any better.

Desperate voices rose around him, shouting, shoving, pushing.

"Let us out!" they shouted.

Men swarmed up the ladder and hammered on the hatch. Others kicked the walls.

Josh stood frozen next to the injured sailor, his mind racing.

"What happened?" the guy groaned, clutching his arm.

"Kamikaze attack, had to be," someone said, his eyes shadowed in the emergency lamplight.

An older man shook his head. "Nope. A sub. Fired a torpedo, I think. More than one. I bet there's a Jap sub down there right now. I bet the Jap captain is celebrating his glorious hit."

Josh thought of his dad, blown to pieces by Japanese bombs. He hated the Japanese. Hated them. If he could, he'd kill every single one of them.

In the bunk room, a doomed silence descended.

Josh looked at the injured sailor. He'd seen the guy before but they'd never spoken. Other guys claimed the kid was a Jap. Uneasily, Josh looked into the sailor's dark, almond-shaped eyes. Was it possible he'd come on board as a Japanese spy? Had this guy secretly broadcast their position to the enemy? Was he the reason they were sinking?

"Are you Japanese?" he blurted.

"No," the young sailor groaned, cradling his injured arm. "I'm not. I was born in Hawaii. My dad was Chinese, my mom's Hawaiian. My name is Lee Wong. It's a good Chinese name. I'm Chinese-American. Okay?"

"Okay," Josh said.

The kid nodded at his bleeding arm. "I gotta bandage this thing. I'm getting kinda lightheaded."

"All right." Nearby, a man lay unmoving. Josh knew he was dead, that he wouldn't need his shirt any longer, but that didn't make him feel any better. Trying not to look, he bent, tore away a section of fabric, and wrapped Lee's bleeding arm.

Blood seeped through the cotton. Lee stared at it ruefully. "If we have to abandon ship, I'm dead."

"What?"

"If the Indy goes down, we'll be in the Philippine Sea. It's full of sharks."

"Sharks?"

"Yeah. Lots of men are injured. The sharks will smell the blood."

Josh grimaced, tried not to picture gnashing jaws and foaming water.

Suddenly that loud voice, that bringer of life and death, came again. "All right, men. Last chance. Get outta here!"

Someone was opening the hatch!

Josh sprang forward, pulling Lee with him. He joined Officer McCoy and the line of uninjured men helping the wounded up the ladder. Josh pushed Lee forward. "Go!" he said. "Get out."

Taut with nerves, wanting to cut and run, he waited his turn, helping the injured first. Ahead of him, boys and men scrambled feverishly up the rungs, diving out the opening.

Then the dreaded warning came again. "Sorry men, that's it!"

"No!"

"We're still in here!"

"Don't close it!"

"You bastards! Don't close it!"

The human chain burst apart as panicked men leaped up the ladder. Josh, already near the top rung, squeezed out the hatch. McCoy was the last one to hurl himself through.

Racing down the corridor, Josh heard the hatch slam shut.

CHAPTER 6

MONDAY JULY 30, 1945
THE PHILIPPINE SEA
00:22 HOURS

THE WARSHIP SHUDDERED, thundering and twisting. Ahead, the corridor was a furnace of flames and smoke. How could Josh reach the main deck when fire blocked his path?

In the distance, wounded men screamed, "Help! Get me out of here!"

To his left, the officers' wardroom door sagged open. Hard to believe he'd been in there half an hour ago, merrily grabbing sandwiches and talking about chocolate cake.

He dove inside and looked around. Hazy smoke made it difficult to see.

A radio operator pushed past him, heading back down the corridor. Must be trying to get to Radio Central, Josh thought. He's trying to get off an SOS.

He choked, coughing and staying low. If he could find a

porthole, he could open it, get some air. He stumbled across the dim room, colliding with the buffet table. Sandwiches and cakes crashed to the floor.

"Stupid table!" he shouted, angry and scared.

"Josh?" a voice rang out. "Over here!"

To his relief, he spotted Lee at an open porthole and ran to join him. Together, they poked their heads out, gulping air. They eyed the dark, churning waves below.

"Sure looks deep," Lee said.

"Yeah."

"And full of sharks."

Josh stared down. He wished this guy would stop talking about sharks. Things were bad enough. Dark rolling swells surged and broke against the hull.

"Like you said, it's a deep ocean. How would sharks know we're here?"

"My dad had a fishing boat. Believe me, they know. They smell blood. From long distances."

"Well, it doesn't matter. We're not abandoning ship. The Captain will keep us afloat until a rescue crew comes."

"Maybe, but unless we find a way up on deck, we're going to choke to death."

Coughing, Josh leaned out further. The guy was right, the smoke was growing thicker by the minute. The blazing corridor wasn't an option. They had only one choice: keep their heads out the window and hope for the best.

Something hit his face. A rope!

He looked up. The rope dangled from a life raft secured high above.

"Let's climb up," he said.

Lee nodded. His face looked strained. "Go for it."

"What's the matter?"

Lee raised his injured arm. "I'm not going anywhere with this."

"Yes, you are. Look, I'll climb up first. Then you tie the rope around your waist and I'll haul you up. Deal?"

Lee said nothing.

With a deep breath, Josh steeled himself and grabbed hold of the porthole's rim. He forced his eyes away from the ocean whirling far below. *Just do it,* he told himself.

He wriggled his shoulders through, then tested the rope with a hard tug. It held. He prayed it would carry his weight. He still didn't have a life vest. If he fell, the ocean would swallow him whole. *Idiot.* If he wanted to live through this, he'd better think harder.

There was a panicked moment as he first hung suspended.

With a determined growl, he started climbing. Hand over hand, inch by inch, swinging left and right, kicking his feet to try and keep from spinning. A final lunge upward took him to a gun mount. He leaped onto the main deck. He'd made it!

The chaos up here was insane.

"Catch!" he shouted, swinging the rope toward Lee.

After what felt like forever, Lee struggled out of the port-hole with the rope knotted around him. Josh started hauling.

Nearby in a slick of bloody water, Chief Pharmacist John Schmeuck knelt amongst a sprawl of badly burned men. Grim-faced, Schmeuck spotted Josh.

"Sailor!" he yelled to him. "Over here! We need life vests!"

The ship rolled, a sickening movement. Josh slid across the deck, still holding the rope. He staggered, then regained his balance. He looked back just in time to see Lee struggle up over the side.

"Sailor!" Schmeuck yelled again. "Get over here. Now! That's an order."

Knife in hand, Josh raced over and hacked until the net holding a clump of life vests gave way. A pile tumbled to the deck. Men pounced on them. Pushing his way in, Josh grabbed an armful.

He began putting a kapok life vest over the head of a badly burned man.

"Get away from me!" the man screamed. "I'm burned! I'm not leaving this fricking ship. There's sharks down there."

Josh pulled the life vest over his own head. He turned to the next injured man. As he handed him a life vest, the ship flipped ninety degrees.

The deck turned into a steel slide.

Josh fell onto his butt and slid toward the railing. Reaching out, he grabbed the lifeline rope. He hung on with all his strength. Down below, the ocean roared by. Ocean spray whipped his face

"Release that lifeboat," a hysterical voice rang out.

Josh clung to his line, watched in disbelief as Lee, Schmeuck, and most of the injured men slid down the deck and smacked into the ocean.

The dark water whirled by, leaving him alone and hanging.

"Abandon ship!" a mighty voice rang out. "Abandon ship! Abandon ship!"

A huge wave crashed over the deck.

It swept Josh overboard and into the hungry sea.

CHAPTER 7

JOSH HIT the water with a stinging belly flop. Down he spiraled, down, down, down into the pitch-dark ocean. Mind spinning, heart racing, he spun around trying to work out which way was up. Dark water surrounded him. He couldn't hold his breath much longer. Which way was up?

He needed air. Needed air. Suddenly, flaying wildly, he reached the surface, only to come face-to-face with the ship's massive, deadly propellers. Thrashing with everything he had, he threw himself backward.

"She'll suck us under," a voice screamed. "Swim! Swim!"

Josh could see sailors still on the vessel, swarming like ants on a stick.

How could this be happening?

The pull of the dying ship sucked him closer. Terrified but

refusing to give in, Josh clawed and kicked. His heavy dungarees hamstrung his legs and his boots felt like anvils. Every stroke was a fight. He was no Olympic swimmer—why on earth had he ever joined the Navy?

The USS Indianapolis groaned and shrieked. Then, in a terrible death plunge, the heavy cruiser disappeared into the dark depths.

Cascades of water crashed over Josh's head, pulling at his limbs, sucking him down all over again. His ears exploded. His eyeballs popped.

All he could hear was the ship, like a dying monster, moaning way down below. He could still see the lights from raging flames glowing through the portholes. They blazed in the lonely darkness as the mighty boat sank toward its watery grave. And he was going with it. Spiraling down. Down.

In a frantic fight, he broke free of its grip and surged to the surface.

A hundred yards away, a man bobbed in the sea.

A man with zombie eyes.

To Josh's confused horror, the man was pulled under. A second later, the sailor's life jacket popped up. Empty.

Suddenly, he saw the shark and he understood.

Its fin cut through the water, began to circle.

Where were the lifeboats? *Where were the lifeboats?*

"Help!" he shouted. "Hey! *Anyone!* Is anyone out there?"

Something bumped his arm and he lurched sideways, heart hammering straight out of his chest. He saw a small crate. Then more floating stuff. Chairs, powder cans, railings, chunks of wood, and poisonous fuel oil littered the ocean.

He began pulling it toward him, praying the junk would confuse the shark. Or at least make it harder for it to get him.

"Lee!" he shouted, wondering if sharks could hear, if calling out was stupid. "Officer Schmeuck! . . . Pete! . . . Is anybody there?"

A wave poured over his head. He shook water from his eyes.

Where was everyone?

With horror, the truth dawned. The whole time the warship was sinking, it had kept moving, plowing rapidly ahead. The survivors would be scattered for miles. He'd seen men jumping. He'd also seen men colliding with the churning, slashing propeller blades. They'd be in the ocean now, bleeding.

He'd been lucky. He hadn't been cut.

He spun slowly, searching for the shark's knife-like fin, but it was nowhere in sight. He breathed out, realizing that the floating junk had given him his first win.

But he'd need a lot more than bits of floating junk to stay alive out here. Hundreds of miles of water surrounded him. It's not like he could swim to safety.

How could the USS Indianapolis—the invincible battleship, the flagship of the US Navy—go down? A floating base, complete with airplane catapults, anti-aircraft guns and cannons, and nearly twelve hundred men on board—how could it be gone, just like that? It seemed impossible. But the Japs had blown her in half and sunk her in less than fifteen minutes.

He struggled to keep hold of his garbage fortress. Shivering in the surging ocean beneath an angry moon, he thought about home. About Mom and Sammy. About his best friends, Jack and Danny, who'd lied to enlist, too. They'd all been torn apart by this war. Would any of them make it back to San Antonio? Would any of them find peace?

He wondered if sharks preferred their food dead or alive. Wondered if it was better to keep still or try swimming, try searching for others, for a life raft. Wondered how long the floating junk would keep them at bay.

In the roaring ocean, he saw no one.

Hours went by. Had the radio operator sent out an SOS? Would anyone come looking for him? Was it possible he was the only survivor?

He longed to spot even one sailor.

Finally, a red sun stained the horizon. In the faint rays, he spied small lumps bobbing above the water. Eyes narrowed, he stared. Prayed.

Then, as the salty swells rose and fell, he made out hundreds of heads.

Men. There were men in the distance.

They were moving. They were alive.

CHAPTER 8

TUESDAY JULY 31, 1945
THE PHILIPPINE SEA
DAY ONE | DAWN

JOSH CALLED OUT, but the men were too far away.

The thought of swimming through shark-infested swells freaked him out, but he had to go for it. The survivors would have rafts. He'd be safe, as long as he made it across the watery distance. It was now or never, for the men were drifting away.

He took a deep breath, then heart racing, moving slowly, he cupped his hands and pulled himself through the water. His water-logged boots made it near impossible. He hated the idea of going barefoot but knew he'd never make it like this. With difficulty, he untied the soggy laces and kicked them off. His sturdy, navy-issue boots sank quickly and were gone.

Freer, he began to move again. In the eerie dawn, every wave peak looked like a shark's fin. Swimming through the thick top layer of fuel oil was like crawling through mud. His eyes, throat, and nose burned. The more oil and saltwater he swallowed, the worse his stomach roiled. He ducked under countless foul waves until he could barely move his arms.

It seemed to take forever to reach the other survivors. A large group of men, eyes jumping with fear and dread, huddled in silence as he joined them. Josh slowly paddled amongst them, trying to spot Lee or Pete or someone he knew.

He passed a group holding an injured friend on their shoulders, struggling to keep the man's badly burned body out of the stinging salt and oil.

A man in a life vest had one arm around a friend without one. "I've got you, Mickey," he said. "You're okay. I've got you!"

So many didn't have life vests. How long could they tread water? Even wearing one, Josh felt half-drowned as waves splashed into his mouth.

A strong arm snaked around his neck. His face went under. He struggled to push free. "What are you doing?"

"I need a vest!" A burly man, his face black with oil shoved up against him. Lips drawn back, like a dog about to bite, he heaved his beefy body up onto Josh.

"Get off of me!" Josh sputtered, trying to keep his head above water. First sharks and now this guy? No way would he hand over his life vest. With all his strength, Josh aimed his knee at the man's crotch and lashed out. Hard. Those years of sports training paid off. Howling with rage, his assailant fell back. Josh swam away, fast.

Up and down the swells he floated. A panicked-looking sailor bobbing beside him stared out at the ocean.

"Swarms of sharks out there," he said, voice trembling. "Hear them? They're going after the dead."

A bolt of terror shot through Josh as he turned and saw the mass of dark fins and frothing water in the distance. He thought of the zombie-eyed man and shuddered. "I saw one. Right in front of me. It bit a guy in half. Ate him right out of his life vest."

"We've got to get the dead away from us," the man said. "The dead are attracting the bastards."

Others agreed. Soon, the call echoed through the survivors. "Move out the dead! Form a circle, men, stay inside. Move out the dead!"

Grim-faced men pushed the bodies of the dead out from the group. Out to sea. Into the Dead Zone.

Josh murmured a prayer for the men who'd died.

"The sharks are afraid of the rest of us," someone said. "They know we'll punch the daylights out of them."

"You hope!"

"We all hope."

"Wishful thinking, pal."

"They can smell blood," a gruff voice whispered nearby.

"Stay away from the wounded if you know what's good for you."

Josh thought of Lee's injured, bloody arm. Was the bandage they'd made enough to stop the bleeding? Had Lee even survived sliding off the deck?

Out loud, he said, "How long do you think before help arrives?"

The gruff-voiced sailor said, "Soon, I reckon. A couple more hours." The man sounded confident, a good sign. "Navy will get the SOS. Or a plane will spot us first. There's a thousand guys floating in the ocean. They'll see us for sure."

Josh nodded. "You're right. No sweat, we'll be visible for miles."

CHAPTER 9

TUESDAY JULY 31, 1945
THE PHILIPPINE SEA
DAY ONE | NOON

NO ONE ARRIVED.

By noon, massive thunder clouds blackened the sky.

The sounds of the sharks doing their dirty work sickened Josh. Where were his friends, Lee and Pete? The guys from his bunkroom? Were they out in the frenzy? Josh floated in the grim circle and tried to believe they were nearby.

People licked their salty lips, their mouths clearly aching with thirst. Josh's were cracked and sunbaked. No one spoke of water or food, though.

Not yet.

Every salt-reddened eye stayed glued to the horizon in hope. But no rescue team came.

Night fell. The blackness made it impossible to see the sharks. How could Josh defend himself if he couldn't see them coming? The sounds of splashing, corpse-shredding rose to a fury. He clapped his waterlogged hands to his ears, clenched his jaws tight.

"Feeding frenzy," the gruff-voiced sailor informed him. "Oceanic whitetips do that. Bet tiger sharks are out there too. They can hear heartbeats."

As lightning ripped the night sky and thunder boomed, Josh pictured the predators cruising the ocean. He pictured their massive grinning mouths and rows of serrated teeth. When the sky opened up and rain fell, he tipped his own head back and drank the falling drops. They rolled down his parched throat, wetting his tongue. Who knew how long they'd be out here?

Who knew if he'd get the chance to drink again?

Josh was dreaming. He was out on the baseball pitch, in the middle of the third inning. The game was tied. His friends that weren't on the field packed the stands. His family was up there too, his Mom and kid brother, his grandparents, even his cousins, aunts and uncles. All of them cheering him on.

Go, Josh! Go, Josh!

Gripping the bat, Josh spotted his dad. Somehow, he was still alive! Dad grinned and held up a huge, hand-drawn sign. *You can do it, son!*

Josh jerked awake at the sound of someone shouting nearby.

He tried to hold onto Dad's image as he blinked in the light.

A blood-red sun bulged along the horizon. A hundred feet away, a fin broke the water's surface. Josh's heartbeat revved to maximum. He could hear it, drumming in his ears. The shark would hear it, too. He started taking deep breaths, closed ranks with the other men, tried to force a calm he couldn't feel.

"He's hunting for more dead," someone said. "Don't worry. Only the dead."

"Yeah, but for how long?" the gruff-voiced man said darkly.

A calm, familiar voice said, "Push the wounded deeper into the center, men. That's what it's after. It can smell the blood. Tighten the circle around them." It was Dr. Haynes.

People started corralling the injured into the group's middle.

A second shark appeared, and then a third.

A sailor said, "Splash, men, kick and splash, it'll scare them off."

Josh doubted anything scared sharks. And the predators were growing bolder now, circling closer.

Where were the life rafts? They needed to get out of the water! Desperately, he scanned the swells. There had to be more than a hundred men in this group. And no sign of a raft. No food. Not a drop to drink.

An empty tin floated by and he grabbed it. With dark clouds still looming, it would surely rain again. He'd use it to catch water. He tucked the can into his life vest and stuck his hands in his armpits to try and keep warm. After the long night, he shook with cold. Guys would be suffering from hypothermia soon.

Something bumped his foot. "Aargh!" he shouted, curling his body up.

"Sorry!" the sailor next to him grunted. "Just my leg."

"Okay," Josh muttered. *I wish I hadn't taken off my shoes. I bet my white feet look like juicy fish. I have to find a life raft!* Eyes narrowed, he scanned for something big and solid bobbing on the cascading blue waves.

"Hey!" a red-haired sailor shouted. "Land! I see land!"

Josh rubbed his salt-encrusted eyes. Land? He saw nothing. The Philippines were hundreds of miles away. But maybe there was an island. Just a small one. Any island would be great.

"Follow me!" The red-haired sailor pointed to the horizon and began swimming hard.

He'd have to swim right through the sharks. Josh watched, picturing a small island. Shady palm trees swaying. Fresh coconuts. It would be wonderful to stand on dry land, to be safe. They could build shelters from palm fronds. Drink coconut milk. He squinted harder. The longed-for island was nowhere in sight.

Four men broke from the pack and followed. Should he join them? Wait, was that red-haired guy Pete? He wasn't sure, every face was covered with fuel oil. Still trying to make up his mind, Josh watched the group swim off, side by side. There was safety in numbers. He'd have to go now.

Then he saw the fins.

The sharks moved fast.

Within seconds, the air filled with blood-curdling screams. "Help! No!"

Red, bloody clouds colored the water.

"They're enormous!" a sailor screamed.

"They're twenty feet," another shouted as a shark veered toward the tightly packed circle.

"Stay together!" Dr. Haynes called out. "Splash! Kick!"

A huge gray shape whooshed under Josh's feet. "Get away," he shouted. "Get away from me!"

Others joined him, shouting, fighting. But more sharks started coming.

"They're after the injured," someone shouted. "Push them to the edge."

Suddenly, a voice said, "Josh! Is that you?"

He turned to see Lee, the whites of his almond-shaped eyes showing in a face covered with oil.

"Lee!" he shouted. Then, as his friend neared, his heart sank. Lee's bandaged arm was dark red. If someone spotted that bloody dressing, Lee would be pushed out. And he didn't even have a life vest.

"Lee!" He grabbed his friend's shoulder, so glad to see a familiar face, and hissed into his ear. "Hide your arm. We've got to get you a life vest."

"From where?"

From the only place one could be salvaged: the Dead Zone. But what choice did they have? "Follow me."

"Are you crazy?" Lee said when he saw where Josh was headed.

"Do you want a life vest or not?"

"When you put it like that," Lee said. "Fine. But I'll go myself."

"No."

Maybe it was crazy, but he didn't care. He'd found a friend and didn't plan to lose him. Swimming past the main group,

Josh waited until a corpse bobbed within reach. Together, they tugged off the lifejacket and shirt. Josh helped Lee struggle into the life vest and wrapped the shirt around Lee's arm. But as they'd worked, the swells had carried them to the group's dangerous outer rim.

With a sharp cry, Lee pointed, and Josh geared himself for attack. Then he saw what Lee was staring at. Something big and floppy floated a ways off. A life raft! Men sat atop it, high and dry.

His hopes of survival soared.

They had to risk it. "We have to get onto that raft."

Lee nodded and spat out a mouthful of greasy water. "But listen to me. I know sharks. I'm from Hawaii, remember? If one grabs you, jab his eyes. Stick your fingers in hard as you can. Punch the nose. Punch the gills. Those are the weak spots."

"Okay."

"Swim slowly. No splashing. Don't draw their attention."

Josh nodded. "All right. Let's do it."

Side by side Josh and Lee half swam, half drifted, moving toward the raft.

CHAPTER 10

TUESDAY AUGUST 1, 1945
THE PHILIPPINE SEA
DAY TWO | MORNING

JOSH REACHED THE RAFT FIRST. It rode the wild swells, much smaller than he'd expected. Good thing he and Lee spotted it early, for it could barely hold the five men already seated there. The men, black with fuel oil, huddled on the balsam wood platform and watched the newcomers with resentful eyes.

Breathing hard, Josh caught hold of a dangling rope. A black-bearded man scowled but grabbed his life vest and hauled him on board.

"Thanks," Josh spluttered, struggling to keep hold of the slippery platform. The raft's center was empty, and he quickly saw why: the latticed wood floor had big gaps. It looked flimsy and water surged through. Not good, with sharks swimming below.

He felt sick and nauseous from swallowing so much gunk. Gagging, he spat out fuel oil and saltwater. Lee was struggling to climb on now. Great. It felt incredible to be out of the ocean.

A bullet-headed sailor heaved himself forward. Josh thought the man would give Lee a hand up.

Instead, he smashed his fist straight into Lee's face.

Horrified, Josh scrambled forward. "What? What are you doing?" he shouted. "What did you do that for?" He leaned out, grabbed his friend's life vest, and tried to haul Lee up.

"We don't want no Jap spies on this raft," Bullet Head snarled.

"He's not a Jap spy!" Josh hung onto Lee's life vest. His friend's nose streamed blood. He had to get him out of the water. He'd attract sharks!

"'Course he's a Jap spy. Look at his slanting eyes," the man sneered.

"He's from Hawaii!" Josh shouted. "He's Chinese-American. His name is Lee Wong. He's my friend."

"Well, go ahead," Bullet Head said. "Jump down and join him, then."

Josh turned to the others for help, but no one met his eyes. He couldn't believe what was happening. How could they act like this? They were all on the same team. All fighting for America.

He searched the five oil-black faces and was shocked to recognize Timmy, a farmer's son. Timmy, he noted, wore just briefs, his chicken-skin legs shaking with cold. The poor guy must have had no time to grab clothes. And he had no life vest.

"Timmy! Come on, help me out," he said. "You know me. I'm Josh. Don't you recognize me?" He swiped the muck from his cheeks. "Lee's not a Jap. And he's bleeding. We need to get him out of the ocean."

"Can't even help myself," Timmy muttered through chattering teeth.

A wave tried to yank Lee from Josh's grip.

"Tie onto this rope," Josh told him. "We'll have to wait until these guys calm down. But if a shark comes, I'm pulling you up, got it?"

Lee fastened the rope to his wrist. "I'm okay."

But Josh knew it was a lie. Lee was bleeding--he was in grave danger. Talk about unfair. Lee was fighting this war, too. He'd volunteered for the Navy. And now his shipmates—men who should have his back—were giving him the shaft because of the shape of his eyes.

The two friends fell silent, watching the ocean.

Like a rollercoaster operated by a maniac, the raft rose and fell in the ten-foot waves. Josh's stomach heaved up and down, up and down. *You're lucky to be on this thing*, he told himself. He could picture his mom saying the same thing. And then telling him to do something useful. Maybe he could find something to help them all. Maybe then they'd feel more friendly and help Lee.

It seemed strange no one had emergency blankets or water cans. Where were the signal mirrors and flares? The survival kits? Surely the raft held supplies? He ran his hands along the sides. Then he gasped as he saw the problem. The float was upside down!

He looked at the men. The bearded guy with his ropy arms and legs seemed most approachable.

"Sir," he said. "I think the raft is upside down."

The officer frowned.

A young, dark-skinned sailor jumped to his feet. "It is!" he shouted. "Look at the floor lattice! It's all twisted. That's why it's broken. The whole thing's flipped."

"I bet there're emergency kits down below," Josh said.

Bullet Head waved his gun. "You check. I'll watch for sharks."

The bearded officer said, "Come with me, son. We'll grab what we can. And the name's Patterson."

"Thanks, Officer Patterson. My friend will help," Josh said.

"Yeah," Lee called. "I'm a good swimmer."

"All right, boys," Patterson said. "Stay alert."

Wary of the deadly, dark-finned predators swarming in the distance, Josh slid into the water. It was strange under the raft. A shadowy world of swirling ocean and small, darting fish.

He soon spotted canvas sacks attached to the siding. He opened one, and a tin of meat fell free and plummeted out of reach. Cursing his mistake, he moved more carefully to fill his arms. The others did the same. When Josh spotted a small first-aid kit, he jammed it into his pocket. He felt guilty but didn't trust the bullet-headed sailor. Lee needed medicine.

He surfaced twice under the lattice for air. Finally, the three swam back out into the blazing afternoon and the dark-skinned sailor hauled Josh aboard. Lee handed up two sacks and started to climb on.

"Not you," Bullet Head growled. "No Jap in my raft."

"Oh, come on, sir," Josh said. "My friend's not a Jap. I told you."

"Shut up."

An engine droned in the distance. Josh was flooded with relief as he spotted a plane. Rescue at last! He couldn't wait to get lifted to safety. He couldn't wait to get away from this creepy guy.

"They've come for us," Timmy yelled, leaping to his feet in his underwear.

"Praise God. The SOS went out!" Patterson growled. "They'll all be here soon. Planes. Tugboats."

Josh sent a silent thanks to the radio operator who'd climbed deep inside the burning ship to send out the SOS.

He joined the others, waving and screaming. Bullet Head fired his gun and the sound boomed in Josh's ears. The pilot would be sure to hear it. The plane roared directly overhead. Josh jumped up and down with excitement, almost overbalancing on the raft's heaving floor. The pilot had seen them!

But then the plane buzzed away.

Flying into the blue sky, it grew smaller and smaller, a speck vanishing over the horizon.

Despair gripped Josh. "He must have seen us. He must have!"

"Blind idiots," a sailor with a thick mustache shouted. "Come back here, you blinking, blind pilots."

Patterson gave a wry laugh.

Josh didn't think it was funny. He glanced at Lee, still

bobbing in the ocean. His friend had been lucky so far, the sharks had stayed away, thrashing and feeding in the distance. But how long before they smelled Lee's blood?

"Sir, can I bring my friend up?" he asked Patterson.

Patterson nodded at Bullet Head's gun. "Nope. You heard the boss."

I was right to keep the medical kit, Josh thought. Bullet Head is nuts. Lee and I may have to leave here. Pray we spot another raft soon.

CHAPTER 11

TUESDAY AUGUST 1, 1945
THE PHILIPPINE SEA
DAY TWO | AFTERNOON

BULLET HEAD STASHED the canvas supply sacks under his legs. The men watched intently as he opened them one by one. Beakers of water. Boxes of malt tablets. Cans of Spam. And, best of all, signal mirrors and a flare rocket.

The dark-skinned sailor opened a beaker of water. Sipped it. And spat. "Full of seawater," he muttered.

Josh groaned and licked his cracked, peeling lips.

Bullet Head handed each man two malt tablets and two crackers. Eagerly, Josh took his and shared half with Lee. He nibbled the wafer. It tasted cheesy and delicious and took away the horrible taste of fuel oil.

As the long day passed, other survivors swam to the raft. Soon angry men filled the platform, all fighting for a spot. Josh had to keep moving out of the way, struggling to keep his space. When the raft was overflowing, other swimmers joined Lee, floating alongside, hanging onto the few dangling ropes.

No one spoke of the horrors they'd seen, but the air smelled of fear.

A massive, gray shadow appeared on the horizon.

"A ship!" a sailor shouted. "A ship!"

Josh's heart thumped fast. After two nights, the Navy was finally coming for them. Relief flooded him. Maybe the pilot had seen them after all. Maybe he'd called the Navy. He leaned over the side and yelled at Lee, "A ship! We'll be on land before you know it!"

Lee, his face sickly, gave a thumbs-up sign.

The ship approached slowly, a submarine-shaped silhouette with a tower on top.

Bullet Head fired his gun.

Josh sent up a flare, the shot's recoil sending him reeling backward. He shouted in triumph as the blazing signal zoomed over the ocean.

"What if it's a Jap ship?" Timmy muttered. "Looks like a

sub. What if it's the same Jap bastards who sank us?"The men muttered. Uneasily, everyone watched to see what it would do.

Like a gray ghost, the ship disappeared.

Choked with disappointment, Josh sat heavily amongst the crush of sunburned, thirsty sailors. His stomach rumbled. Suddenly he had a happy thought. He still had the egg and mayo sandwiches wrapped in waxed paper! And the chocolate cake. They'd be soaked but still edible. He'd forgotten all about them!

He dug into his dungaree pockets and hauled out a squashed package. Opening it, he scraped out a section of wet bread and mashed up egg and mayo, surprised it hadn't dissolved. Bullet Head watched with narrowed eyes. Josh knew he'd have to share, so he carefully dug out more bread and the crumbly chocolate cake. The slick icing looked so good. He licked his dry lips as he separated a small portion for himself, intending to hand some of this treasure over the side to Lee and offer the rest to the others.

Standing slowly, Bullet Head stretched. Then he reached out and grabbed the lot. He grinned at Josh. A shark-like grin that never reached his eyes.

CHAPTER 12

TUESDAY AUGUST 1, 1945
THE PHILIPPINE SEA
DAY TWO | LATE AFTERNOON

BY LATE AFTERNOON, the sun broiled the raft, burning faces and bodies. Out here, it was easy to feel like the world no longer existed. That there was only this deadly ocean. So he forced himself to think of home. Crazy to think how he and his friends had played pirates when they were kids, making each other walk the plank into a fake sea with pretend sharks waiting below. If only he could pretend this was all some lousy game . . . If only he could call it quits and go in for dinner.

For the moment, at least, the sharks had disappeared. Not a fin in sight. Instead of relief, though, it unsettled him.

The raft had floated clear of the fuel spill. The ocean sparkled in every direction, cool and tempting. He was so thirsty. His tongue was swollen, his voice hoarse. How long could you go without water? Somewhere he'd read four days, maybe a week. The sea sure looked inviting. He saw the other men eyeing it, too.

"How bad can it be? Should be safe to have a few sips," Bullet Head grunted, leaning to dip his hand in the water.

"No!" warned a bowlegged, older man. "Don't do it. Saltwater makes you crazy."

"How would you know? You're crazy already." Bullet Head grinned as he scooped a handful of saltwater into his mouth. "Tastes better than a pint of beer."

A few others took a gulp.

"Tastes fine," someone shouted.

"Better than dying of thirst," someone else agreed.

"It'll make you even more thirsty," the bowlegged sailor muttered.

"I'm just having a sip," Timmy said. "It's not so bad."

Josh wondered if they were right. His cracked lips stung and his tongue stuck to the roof of his dry mouth. How bad could a few drops be? If they weren't saved soon, he'd risk it.

The day lasted forever. At sunset, the sharks returned. This time they came close, circling the raft.

"Bastards!" Patterson shouted, his voice cracking. "Creepy bastards!" He reached into his dungarees and produced a lethal-looking knife. "Wait 'till I get you. Slit your throats, I will."

A scrawny sailor with grizzled hair grabbed a can of Spam from under Bullet Head's legs and gave a shout of triumph. "Spam! Let's eat, boys."

With a roar of approval, the men crowded forward, reaching out. Bullet Head scowled but did nothing.

The scrawny sailor ripped off the Spam lid and scooped out pink meat. The closest men shuffled and pushed for a bite.

The Spam smelled wonderful. Josh felt his dry mouth watering.

"No. No!" Eyes flashing terror, Patterson grabbed the can and flung it far into the ocean.

Too late.

As Patterson shouted a warning, Josh saw it, a massive white dorsal fin slicing through the ocean toward them.

Beside him, the bowlegged sailor groaned. "A white tip! Smelled the Spam. God save us." He stood and shouted to the men in the ocean. "Prepare yourselves, boys! A monster's headed our way."

Josh stared in horror.

The massive shark torpedoed toward them.

CHAPTER 13

"IT SMELLS THE SPAM," the grizzled sailor shouted. "Splash, men! Kick!"

"Move!" Lee warned the men in the ocean. "Get out of the way! It's coming fast."

The desperate swimmers paddled wildly to the raft's far side. A few managed to force their way on top, falling onto those already on board.

The shark reached the flimsy raft and began to circle. Then, like a gentle, curious giant, it began to nudge the corners, seeming almost friendly. A spooky gray shape, it dove under and carefully poked at the floor's broken lattice.

It's playing with us, Josh thought. Tormenting us. It knows what it's doing. It's the hunter. We're the prey. And we've nowhere to go.

Suddenly the shark disappeared.

Anxiously, the men scanned the water. There was no sign of the creature. Josh breathed a sigh of relief. Maybe it was going after the can of Spam down below.

Without warning, the shark's giant pointed snout shoved through the broken wood lattice.

"Pull your legs up!" someone yelled. "Lie flat on your backs."

The men on the raft bunched on the balsam wood platform. Panicked men in the ocean began to sob. With a warrior scream, the dark-skinned sailor kicked the snout. The shark retreated. But it returned immediately. Rising up again, thumping at the latticework.

Josh could see the creature. It looked at least fifteen feet long. Incredible. Magnificent. Deadly. Rippling muscles under armored skin. Cold eyes filled with determination. The shark was determined to get in. To sink them all for good.

The dark-skinned sailor pulled a knife out of his holster. Fast as a whip, he stabbed the creature in the eye. "Got you!" he yelled. "I'm going to drink your blood, you sucker!"

Wild with pain and fury, the shark lashed out, slamming the raft with its leathery tail.

Screaming hysterically, the men crashed to the other side, falling on top of one another.

Josh, lying with his legs curled on the edge, lost his grip. Arms flailing wildly, he tried to find something to cling to. Within seconds, he was over the side and in the ocean, right beside the shark.

The creature eyeballed him. Flat, cold eyes.

It was so big. So unbelievably enormous.

I'm going to be eaten alive, he thought.

Rough, scaly skin sandpapered his arm. His brain fired on all cylinders. He had to act. If he didn't, he'd die.

"Jab the eyes!" he heard Lee scream. "Jab the eyes!"

Josh stuck his hand out blindly, feeling the creature's tough, scaly head. Where were its eyes? And then he felt a soft patch. An eye? He jabbed two fingers in as hard as he could.

The shark whirled around and dove down. With a thrill of triumph, Josh watched him go. "How'd you like that, sucker?" he shouted. "Got you in your good ole juicy eye."

Thrilled with his success, he clawed his way back to the raft.

As he tried to climb up and over the rim, Bullet Head pushed him down. "Get! Get away from us! Look at your arm, boy! You're bleeding like a stuck pig. You're shark bait."

Stunned. Too exhausted to argue, Josh joined Lee, hanging on to a line in the ocean.

Lee ripped at the edge of his shirt with his teeth and managed to tear off a strip. He wrapped it tightly around Josh's arm. But the makeshift bandage was soon red. As red as the bandage around Lee's arm. Together, they were definitely shark bait.

The men floating alongside the raft eyed them nervously and moved as far from them as they could.

Josh didn't blame them. How long, he thought, before they tell us to go?

When night fell, he pulled out the emergency kit, glad to have ointment for Lee and himself. But when he opened the tin, he saw it wasn't medical supplies. Instead, it held fishing hooks and lines. He popped it back in his dungaree pocket. Not what he'd thought, but who knew when he might be glad to have it.

CHAPTER 14

WEDNESDAY AUGUST 2, 1945
THE PHILIPPINE SEA
DAY THREE | NOON

THE RELENTLESS SETTING sun burned down on Josh's head. Even with his eyes closed, he could see its glare. The ocean sparkled, fresh, inviting, still as a lagoon. With no sharks in sight, men slid from the raft into the cool water, first splashing it on their heads and then sipping it defiantly.

Again, Josh wondered if he should risk it. Did saltwater really drive a man mad? Well, he'd find out soon as more and more men gulped it down.

Alongside Josh, a grizzled sailor dove and resurfaced, eyes rolling. "I had a drink! It's down there, friends. The ship's just down below. With all the water you can drink."

Was it true? For a moment, Josh almost believed it. Maybe he should dive down, see for himself.

"That's not possible," said a skeptical voice.

"You're lying," shouted Patterson, leaning over the side of the raft.

"Do you remember the scuttlebutt?" the grizzled sailor roared. "The one with lots of cold water? I dove down and turned it on, guys. It works. The water is fresh. Fresh. I'll show you! Follow me!"

Sobbing, a lost look in his eyes, Timmy plunged in. Other hysterical men followed, diving down to find the ship. Some even pulled off their life jackets before diving.

Could it possibly be true? Josh looked over at Lee, who licked his salt-white lips and shook his head.

"We saw the ship go down," Lee croaked. "It's too deep by now. There's no way we could reach it."

A wide-eyed sailor popped up, shouting, "There's pretty girls down there! Lots of them!"

"It's the saltwater," Lee said. "They're going crazy."

"There's a Jap over there," a man cried. "He's trying to kill me."

"Get the Jap! Kill him!" Screaming men, foaming at the mouth, turned on each other.

Were they after Lee?

In a panic, Josh spun, ready to fight for his friend. But thankfully no one was looking at Lee. Some other poor man was being attacked. The saltwater really was turning the men crazy.

Head throbbing, Josh watched in mounting horror. The scene grew worse and worse. Most sailors had knives, and now the knives were drawn. This was turning into a blood-bath. And he and Lee would be right in the middle!

He felt his calf, checking his blade was still in its holster. It was. Not much of a weapon, he thought, but I'm glad I have it.

A burly man with red eyes shoved his face right up to his. "Give me some of your water," he shouted.

Josh paddled backward. "I don't have water."

"You do. You're hiding it."

"I don't! I swear!"

The man shouted right in his face, his breath rancid, his face red with sunburn and fury. "I want some of that water, boy! And you're going to give it to me!" Looking around, he yelled. "Hey! Hey guys. This sneaky fella's got the beaker."

Three men, bobbing in their life vests, scowled at Lee and Josh.

"I don't have water," Josh shouted. "The beaker was cracked. Empty."

The men swam nearer. This wasn't looking good.

A voice rang out, the voice of authority. "No one has water, men. Just stay strong. Help will be here soon."

Marine Captain Parke! Josh thought. At last, an officer was here! Maybe Parke could control the men.

"Don't drink the saltwater. It'll make you mad," Parke

shouted. "Won't be long before the Navy finds us, men. Tie your life vests together. Stay together. You don't want to drift away."

Good idea, Josh thought. He and Lee tied their vests together, bobbing side by side. Parke's voice reminded him of his dad. He felt a pang of longing. Dad was a good person to have around in a bad situation.

He remembered how once he, Dad, and Sammy had gone for a hike down a country road. A furious Doberman, teeth bared, charged through an open farm gate and cornered them, mean and growling, ready to attack.

"Back!" Dad ordered, his voice loud and firm. "Back! Down, boy! Down!"

Then he'd spoken softly to Josh. "Hold Sammy's hand and move away slowly. Don't run. Don't look into its eyes."

That's what these men were like now. Mad dogs. "Stay away from them," he whispered to Lee. "Don't look at their eyes. Let's swim behind the raft, get out of their way."

Clutching the line, Josh eyed the knot of defiant sailors who kept drinking saltwater. Parke's warning was right. The water was affecting them. Aghast, he watched as two men, mouths foaming, held their struggling friend underwater. The air filled with screams. The terrible fight went on and on. Soon, the bodies of dead and injured sailors littered the sea.

"Sharks," Lee groaned, pointing. "Look!"

Josh stared out to sea. Hundreds of black fins knifed through the water toward the raging group. The sharks, attracted by their blood and urine, were coming in for the kill. They attacked in a fury.

With a sick feeling, Josh listened for Parke's voice. For a while he could hear it bellowing orders, shouting warnings, trying to get the hysterical men back to the safety of the raft.

Josh's heart pounded. Why didn't Parke return to the raft and save himself? Then suddenly, Parke's voice went silent.

The sharks ate for hours. Every bump on Josh's leg felt like a shark. He longed to be sitting on the raft but didn't dare challenge Bullet Head and his gun. Hang in there, he told himself. Help will arrive. Soon. Surely soon.

High in the sky, another plane passed over. And then another. Josh and Lee and the men around him waved furiously.

But no one noticed.

CHAPTER 15

A BARREL BOBBED PAST.

"Hey! We can ride that thing," Lee shouted.

Josh looked at the bloody ocean, at the screaming, fighting men. He nodded. "Yeah. Let's get away from this crazy bunch."

Moving slowly but surely, they swam after the barrel. The hissing wind and rising waves struck Josh's face, pushing him back. He thought he heard jabbering. Were the crazed sailors after him? Trying to kill him? Trying to take his life vest?

He spun, but no one was following. He went to swim after Lee but couldn't see him. The barrel had disappeared too. All he could see were the endless swells, the breaking waves.

His soggy life vest had lost most of its buoyancy. Now his nose was only a few inches above the water. He ran his swollen tongue over his cracked lips and groaned. Perhaps a little sip wouldn't hurt. He scooped a handful of water and brought it to his lips.

"Don't!" Lee's voice rang out. "How would your mom feel if you went crazy?"

He groaned. "Yeah . . . you're right." He pictured his mom. She'd ask why he'd done such a dumb thing. Tears filled his eyes. He longed to see her face. Even if it was an angry face.

Mom must be so mad that he'd forged her signature on the permission form. *If I hadn't done that, I wouldn't be here now. Dying here now.* He squeezed his eyes shut. He loved his mom and little brother so much. He missed them. What was he doing here at all? He must have been crazy. What good had he thought he could do?

He'd wanted to fight the Japs. What a joke. The Japs had sure ended that plan fast. They'd sunk his ship, the beautiful Indy, before he'd had a chance to fight at all. Now he was probably going to die. To drown. To end up as some shark's dinner. Part of the whole dead-sailor-buffet.

He should have stayed home, should have been there for Sammy. He pictured his kid brother. So skinny and full of energy. Just like himself at Sammy's age, all long, knobby legs and long, scrawny neck. *Bones*, they'd called Josh at school. In third grade, some joker named him that, and it stuck.

He'd filled out later. Playing baseball and running track had done that. He should be at home right now playing catch with Sammy.

"Where's the barrel?" he shouted to Lee. "Thought you'd be riding it off into the sunset."

"I wish," Lee said. "Damn thing's moving fast."

They'd lost the barrel? What were they going to do now?

"Wait here," Lee croaked. "I'll try and get it."

"No way. I'm not waiting here."

The swells were growing. Low black clouds hung in the sky. Darkness was coming fast. Both of them were injured. They hadn't eaten or drank for days. On the raft, Josh had thought things couldn't get much worse. But now they were lost.

Then, as he rose up on a swell, he spotted what looked like a makeshift raft. For a moment, he couldn't believe it. A thrill of pure relief ran through him.

"Lee! Raft!" he stammered. "Over there!"

Lee whooped and they struck out, swimming as hard as they could. The raft meant the difference between life and death. No way would they let it drift off.

Puffing hard, they reached the makeshift float. Someone had lashed together two ammunition cans and three potato crates. Swimming closer, Josh saw a pair of sailors. One young guy about his age, his face bright red with sunburn, and an older man, his face peeling and his eyes bloodshot. I must look like that too, Josh thought, touching his stinging nose.

Both men shouted a greeting and leaned down to pull them up. The top of the raft was soft and dry, lined with kapok life vests. As Josh sank into the kapok, he gave a big sigh.

"Thank you," he said.

Thank heavens these men were friendly and not throwing him and Lee overboard.

"I'm Chris." The older sailor shook their hands, his eyes warm and creased. "We saw you guys swimming for us. Glad you made it."

"Hi! I'm Paul," said the young sailor, a freckled guy with a tattoo of the Indy on his right arm.

Josh and Lee introduced themselves. They pulled off their sodden kapok life vests, squeezed them and laid them out to dry. Josh winced as he touched the blisters on his shoulders. It felt great to be free of the vest for a while.

Paul dug into one of the barrels and handed them each a rotten potato. Gratefully, Josh picked off the skin and the stinking, rotten parts, and slowly ate what was left. His stomach rumbled, still empty. It had been days since his last meal. Blinking, he looked around the raft, saw a broken paddle and some tin cans.

Suddenly, he remembered the fishing kit. He took it out, flipped up the lid.

"Is that what I think it is?" Chris said.

"Yep."

"Good man," Chris said.

Josh threaded a nylon line on to a hook. He handed the kit to Chris, who began assembling a line, too. Maybe they'd have fish for lunch!

"When do you think they'll come for us?" Paul said.

"Soon," Josh replied, watching the fishing line dangling in the ocean.

"I don't know," Paul said. "Something's gone badly wrong. If Navy Command knew the USS Indianapolis had gone down, they'd be here by now."

Josh said nothing but Paul's words rang true. It was what he feared, what he'd tried not to think. How long could they last out here? They had to hang on. And hanging on was hard when you'd lost all hope.

He could hear Dad's voice. *If you give up hope, you're dead.*

"We're going to die," Paul groaned.

You could talk yourself into giving up and dying. It would almost be easier. But he didn't want to die. Maybe he could talk himself into living.

"We're going to live," he told Paul. "We're not going to die. We're going to make it. Don't quit. Hang on."

He could almost hear Dad's voice telling him to never quit.

Had it really been three years ago that Dad, a Navy mechanic, received his transfer notice? At dinner, he'd told the family he was being sent to the Pacific Fleet Naval base at Pearl Harbor, Hawaii.

Josh, his mom, and his little brother heard the news in dismay. Although World War II was raging in Britain and Europe, American troops were not part of the battle. Life was peaceful in Josh's home town of San Antonio.

"Why?" Mom said. "America isn't at war."

Dad looked solemn. "It's only a matter of time before America joins the fight. The warships I'll be maintaining will be a big part of the action. America has to fight the German aggression. We have to fight for freedom. Sometimes you have to fight for what you believe in."

Josh was filled with pride. It sounded so exciting.

But it wasn't. Dad died when the Japanese bombed Pearl Harbor. Thousands of Americans died.

Before leaving, his father had said, "If I die, take care of your mom. And your little brother. Okay, son? You'll be the man of the family."

He'd promised. Yes. He'd take care of Mom and Sammy.

Now, guilt filled him because if he died out here, he'd fail to keep that promise.

Of course, his mother could take care of herself. She could probably take care of the whole Navy. But she'd be alone with both her men gone. Dead and gone. What if Germany and Japan combined forces? What if they attacked the very heartland of America? Who would defend Mom and Sammy then?

Chris, his creased blue eyes watching the ocean, patiently dangled his fishing line over the side of the raft. Every now and again, he glanced at Josh. Eventually, he spoke. "Deep thoughts, lad?"

Josh nodded.

"Sometimes you just have to do the best you can," Chris said.

"I guess."

"I'll take care of you guys for as long as I can," Chris said.

Paul looked up. "What makes you think you can take care of us?"

"Because I'm a Marine, I'm tougher than hell."

Paul laughed. Josh was glad to see he looked better, less dejected, more hopeful. "Well, I'm a farmer from Minnesota," Paul said. "That makes me tougher than you."

"Could be," Chris said. "Right now, I'm trying to catch us a fish for dinner. And I have a few fish down here that might be interested in my bait."

Josh slid over with his line. He watched, stomach rumbling, as hundreds of small fish circled his bait. Did fish even eat rotten potato? It looked like they might.

The fish were pretty, bright yellow with black stripes. Almost too pretty to eat. How great it would be if they could catch one! His last real meal had been so long ago that his stomach thought his throat was cut.

Lee slid over and joined them. "We have those fish in Hawaii too," he said. "They're good to eat. Small but tasty. They're called Tang. See the black spot near their tails? It's a fake eye. Makes the fish seem bigger than it is. Or that's what the fish like to think."

Josh laughed, feeling a small moment of delight. There were wonderful things in the world. He just needed to make sure he lived long enough to see them. Well, don't quit, he told himself. People have survived for months on rafts. We could live on fish and rainwater. We could hold on for a long time.

"So where are you two from?" Chris asked.

"I'm from San Antonio," Josh said.

"Ah, San Antonio. Love that river." Chris smiled. "And that great fort. The Alamo. Do you know about the battle of the Alamo, son? Do you know how Davy Crockett fought there? How he fought for Texas?"

Josh nodded. "I sure do." His heart gave a momentary twinge, but it was a happy memory. His family had gone when he was little to see the Alamo fort and hear the story of Davy Crockett. That was one brave man, Davy Crockett, king of the wild frontier.

At the fort gift shop, they'd bought him a Davy Crockett fur hat. He'd worn it for months, refusing to go anywhere without it. He even wore that hot, sweaty hat to bed. He smiled at the thought.

When he got home, he'd buy Sammy a Davy Crockett hat. He'd tell him about Davy and his small group of brave soldiers who fought to the end and never quit. He and Sammy could shout the rousing battle cry *Remember the Alamo!*

Chris turned to Lee. "And you, son?"

"I'm from Hawaii," Lee said.

"Born in Hawaii, huh?"

Oh no . . . Not again. Josh knew why Chris was asking. What if Chris decided Lee was Japanese? What if he decided he was a spy and ordered him off the raft?

"Lee's Chinese-American," Josh said, stepping quickly into the conversation. "His grandparents came from China."

For a long minute, Chris studied Lee. Then he nodded. "I've never been to Hawaii. Must be a nice place."

"It is," Lee replied.

"Too bad the Japanese bombed it," Chris said. "Too bad they bombed Pearl Harbor. Lots of my mates died."

"I know. It was awful," Lee replied.

Josh didn't like the way the conversation was going. He had no way to prove that Lee was Chinese-American. What if Chris didn't believe him?

"Those Japanese planes just came in out of the blue and bombed our men," Chris muttered. "Why would people do something like that?"

Lee shook his head. Josh saw that his face had grown red.

Chris turned back to his fishing line, carefully attaching a piece of potato to the fishing hook. He sat silently, watching the ocean swells.

Josh and Lee sat silent too. *What was Chris thinking?*

It was late afternoon, feeding time for the sharks. On the horizon, swarms gathered. Josh could see their fins. The wind and waves were carrying the raft across the ocean in what Chris said was a northerly direction. Soon they'd be far from Dr. Haynes' large group of survivors. If Lee was kicked off the raft here, what would they do?

Miles in the distance, something glinted. Josh leaped to his feet as rays from the setting sun caught the metal of a plane.

Then signal flares, faint plumes of smoke, rose from the sea. There were other survivors out there. A third group. And they had emergency flares! Josh's hopes soared. Surely the pilot would see that!

He watched, tense his eyes burning as he peered into the distance.

The plane circled. His hopes rose.

Then they crashed as the plane, like all the planes, disappeared into the sky.

CHAPTER 16

THURSDAY AUGUST 3, 1945
THE PHILIPPINE SEA
DAY FOUR | MORNING

"JOSH?" Lee said, talking softly. "I need to tell you something."

"What?" Josh turned reluctantly. He didn't want to hear bad news. He wanted to stay determined. Upbeat. Was Lee going to confirm what he already feared? That they had almost no chance of ever being spotted by a plane? That a man's head bobbing in the ocean was the size of a bobbing coconut? That a small raft was invisible to a pilot miles high in the clouds?

Lee motioned him away from Chris, who was dozing in the dawn light.

Josh looked uneasily at his friend. Lee looked weird.

"I lied to you," Lee whispered. "I'm sorry, Josh. My name isn't Lee Wong. My father wasn't Chinese."

Josh stared at him. "What's your real name? And if you're not Chinese, what are you?"

Had Bullet Head been right? Was Lee a Japanese spy? Josh's brain felt scrambled. *What if Lee had signaled the Indy's position to the Jap sub?*

"My name is Lee Tanaka." Lee's voice trembled. "I'm so sorry, I shouldn't have lied. But I thought you wouldn't help me."

"So, you're Japanese?"

"Not Japanese. I'm Japanese-American," Lee said. "My grandfather was Japanese. He came from Japan to Hawaii years ago to work in the sugarcane fields. My dad was born in Hawaii. He was Japanese-American. And he wasn't a spy. I'm not a spy, I swear it. My dad died in France, fighting in this war. He volunteered to fight." There were tears in Lee's eyes. He dashed them away with his hand and wiped his nose. His face was scrunched with emotion.

"Okay." Josh glanced at the two other men on the raft. No one was listening. Chris was snoring and Paul was softly singing the Navy hymn, beating time with the broken oar on a tin can.

Not knowing what to say, Josh sat silent.

Paul kept singing. He was fudging some of the words, and his tune was shaky, but the song was beautiful. "Oh hear us when we cry to thee," Paul sang, "for those in peril on the sea."

Somehow, hearing the song soothed Josh's soul. "It's okay," he told Lee. "Let's not talk about it now."

It would be bad if Chris and Paul heard that Lee was Japanese. Who knew how they'd react? Maybe they'd act like Bullet Head. Josh couldn't picture them like that, but he couldn't take the chance.

He felt strange about Lee being Japanese. Lots of Americans were suspicious of Japanese-Americans. They feared they were spies. That's why so many had been interned in isolation camps. Because they weren't trusted. Could he trust Lee? Lee had lied to him.

"I understand if you don't trust me," Lee stammered. "My father's fighting unit, the 442nd Infantry Regiment, fought hard for America. When he died, I joined the Navy to fight in his name."

"I do trust you," Josh said. He realized that even though Lee had lied, he understood why. And he did trust him. He nodded gravely at his friend. "Of course I trust you. How many times have you helped me and even saved my life?"

"You saved mine," Lee said.

"I also joined the Navy because my father died," Josh said. "Are you under seventeen, too? Did you forge your mom's signature on the Navy permission form?"

Lee nodded. "Yeah. I sort of wish I hadn't."

Josh gave a hollow laugh. "Me too."

"So you're also sixteen?" Lee asked.

"Yeah. It would be just as bad out here if we were eighteen though!"

"But we'd have lived a couple more years," Lee said, wistfully. "We might have had girlfriends. I've never even kissed a girl. Not properly, anyway."

"Maybe it would've been harder, then," Josh said. "All those sobbing girls."

Lee laughed. "Yeah. Wish I'd had a chance to own a car. That would have been good. I was looking forward to driving my first car. A little convertible. With the top down."

"Still time," Josh said.

He wondered if that was true.

CHAPTER 17

THURSDAY AUGUST 3, 1945
THE PHILIPPINE SEA
DAY FOUR | MORNING

JOSH LOOKED out at the empty ocean. He felt awkward. He wished Lee had never told him he was Japanese. He hated the Japanese.

Chris had woken and taken up his fishing line.

"Why has no one come to save us, do you think?" Lee said.

"They will. They must realize by now something's wrong. They'll come soon," Josh said.

"I wonder if the Navy has told our families that we're missing," Lee said.

Josh pictured his mother's worried face. God, he hoped they hadn't told her. He imagined Mom getting the telegram. *We regret to inform you that your son is missing in action.* He felt so guilty. He loved his mom so much.

When they'd heard about the Pearl Harbor attack, Josh had

been in the yard fixing the brakes on his bike. The radio had been blaring out *Oh Susanna,* a song he liked, when an announcer interrupted the broadcast.

The radio announcer's voice was grim. "There's been an air raid on Pearl Harbor. This is not a drill."

He raced into the kitchen. "Mom!" he shouted. "There's been an air raid. The Japanese bombed the Naval base at Pearl Harbor!"

The USS Arizona burning at Pearl Harbor

His mom came running from the bedroom. She clutched the kitchen table and stood for a long moment, simply staring out of the window. Then, all day, he and his mom waited together, sick with anxiety, hunched over the radio, desperate for news.

The following day, the United States declared war on Japan. Clinging together, he and his mom listened as President Roosevelt spoke to the nation.

"The attack yesterday on the Hawaiian Islands has caused severe damage to American naval and military forces," the President said. "I regret to tell you that very many American lives have been lost."

Day after day, they waited for news. They had no idea if Dad was alive or dead or lying somewhere injured. As news broadcasts grew more detailed, his hatred for the Japanese grew.

"Dive bombers, high-level bombers, and torpedo planes tore the harbor apart," the radio announcer reported. "More than twenty-four hundred Americans have been killed, more than a thousand injured. The US Pacific Fleet has been decimated, twenty-one Pacific Fleet ships have been sunk or damaged, seventy-five percent of planes were damaged or destroyed."

Josh pictured the men fighting back as planes roared over and bomb after bomb hit the battleships. He imagined his dad fighting and felt sick with dread. He knew his dad would fight to the max. Dad would defend others. What were the chances that he was alive and uninjured?

For weeks, still no news came. No word if Dad was alive or dead. For endless nights, he listened as Mom prayed. Every time someone knocked on the front door, he and his mom cringed, expecting the dreaded telegram announcing that Dad had been killed.

And then, their worst fears came true. The telegram arrived. Dad had indeed been killed. He'd died in the fiery waters of Pearl Harbor during the second wave of Japanese bombs.

He hated the Japanese. Hated them. He'd joined the Navy to fight them. To avenge his father. But he didn't hate Lee. How could he? Lee was his friend. It wasn't Lee's fault Japan had gone to war against the United States. Lee was American. And Lee's own father died in the war.

He stole a quick look at Lee. His friend looked depressed. Josh felt an unexpected pang of sympathy. He guessed that after the attack at Pearl Harbor, it would be hard to be Japanese-American.

A commotion rose on the other side of the raft. Chris beamed widely as he reeled in his line. "A bite!" he yelled. "Look! Caught one!"

Josh and Lee jumped up. A big silver-blue fish dangled from the hook. "That's an ono!" Lee shouted. "That's a good fish! The word *ono* means good in Hawaiian!" He laughed. "That's how good that fish is! I'll slice it real thin with my knife. I'll turn it into sashimi. It'll be real, real good!"

Josh heard his stomach rumble. He was starving. Imagine Chris catching a really tasty fish! A fish would be juicy, not hard to swallow. He licked his lips. His spirits lifted. They really could survive out here!

Eyes narrowed in concentration, Chris reeled in his flapping catch.

He yelled triumphantly and tossed it into the raft as a shark leaped up out of the ocean. With one snap, it swallowed the fish, seeming to hover in the air for a brief, shocking second.

Then, the massive beast thumped onto the flimsy raft.

Right at Josh's feet.

CHAPTER 18

THURSDAY AUGUST 3, 1945
THE PHILIPPINE SEA
DAY FOUR | NOON

JOSH LEAPED BACK as the raft rocked and swayed. Chris fell, landing on his hands and knees. Lee and Paul reeled back, gasping in shock.

The shark, at least a ten-to-twelve-foot oceanic whitetip, thrashed furiously. Blood from the ono dripped from its knife-like teeth.

"Get it off!" Paul screamed.

Josh grabbed the broken oar and swung it at the shark's head.

The shark lifted its chinless face and heaved itself forward.

Paul shrieked and fell against Josh.

Again Josh struck.

"Grab its tail!" Chris yelled. With a blood-curdling yell, he jumped onto the thrashing body. "Stay away from the teeth!"

Josh followed with Lee. Together they grappled with the powerful creature. Strong muscles moved and rippled under Josh's arms, its sandpaper hide tearing at Josh's skin. He pulled as hard as he could. They had to get the enormous, thrashing creature off the raft. Already, they were sinking. They'd land in the ocean with the rest of the sharks.

"Pull!" Chris yelled. "On three. *One, two, three!"*

Josh pulled with all his might. But there was no way to control the shark. The mighty monster snapped its jaws. Lashed its powerful tail. With an incredible heave, it rocketed forward. Chased off the raft and into the ocean.

They'd done it! The shark was gone.

Chris let out a triumphant yell.

The raft tipped.

Screaming, the four men plummeted into the water.

Josh hit the water hard. Gasping, he kicked to the surface. In a blur of horror he saw the shark, its leering face beside him, its mouth wide open. The razor-like teeth latched on to his life vest.

Down, the shark dove, rolling and twisting. And down Josh went. He shoved hard. The creature refused to let go.

Frantic, he reached to pull his knife from the calf-holster. The eye! He had to get it in the eye. Furiously, he jabbed at the beast. The blade connected with shark-skin, gritty as sandpaper, solid as armor. With a viselike grip, the shark held on, jerking its head.

Then Lee was beside him, diving at his side, jabbing the creature's head, trying to get at the eyes too.

The shark was big. So big. A massive dark-gray body pulling him down. To a watery grave. This was the shark's world. Here, the shark was king. Josh fought hard but could feel himself weakening. He needed air. His lungs were bursting.

The shark jerked its head from side to side. Then it let go of the life vest.

For a moment, a wonderful moment, Josh was free.

Then the shark latched on to his arm.

First, he felt nothing. Just the pressure of something hard wrapped around his forearm. Then he saw the blood, his blood, turning the swirling ocean red. All it would take was one good jerk for the monster to tear it off.

Well, it wasn't going to win. Josh became a raging fury. With his good arm, he swung his knife at it again and again.

Lee was still with him, heading straight for the shark from the front. The shark let go of Josh and opened its huge mouth wider. The shark and Lee were face to face.

Hot with fear and fury, Josh buried the blade deep in the shark's gills.

The spiraled away.

Lungs heaving, Josh kicked his way up to the surface. He swam hard for the raft, gulping air. Chris grabbed him and hauled him on board.

Time stood still as Josh stared at his arm. Blood streamed, covering the floor. Wow, he thought, my blood really is red. Very red.

Lee scrambled into the raft after him. He pressed his hand on the wound, holding it tight. "Make a tourniquet," he shouted.

Chris tore a strip from his shirt and wound it around and around, tying it tight. Still, blood covered the floor. The blood would attract more sharks. More hungry sharks, smelling the feast.

Lightheaded, Josh watched, as if somewhere above it all. "Hey, Lee," he said. "I went for the gills. I turned him into sashimi."

And then he passed out.

CHAPTER 19

THURSDAY AUGUST 3, 1945
THE PHILIPPINE SEA
DAY FOUR | LATE AFTERNOON

HALF-CONSCIOUS, Josh lay on the bobbing raft. He felt dizzy and weak. He'd lost a lot of blood. Was this what it felt like to die? If he died, maybe he'd see Dad. Did that happen? Was it like the pastor said? Did you meet your loved ones in heaven? He hoped so.

Sometimes you've got to fight for what you believe in. That's what Dad had said. Well, he believed in fighting to stay alive. To get home.

He sat up, confused. He'd been out of it. Really out of it. He shivered. His arm throbbed. It felt huge and hot.

"We'll never get out of here," Lee groaned.

"Yes, we will," Josh managed. "We've hung on for days. You're going to drive that sports car in Hawaii."

Hang in there, he told himself. Don't lose it now. Eyes half-open, he saw a bright white light. For a moment, he thought he was looking at heaven.

A buzzing sound came from overhead.

"A plane," Chris shouted. "A plane!"

Then Josh saw it, a bomber, high above. But instead of leaving, this plane banked. It began to circle. Did that mean . . . Yes! The pilot had seen them. Finally. *Finally!*

Josh reached to high-five Lee, Paul, and Chris.

Breathless they watched the plane's hatch yawn open. First, life vests rained down. Then kegs of water crashed into the ocean, barely missing the raft. The kegs landed hard. And split.

An SB-29 drops a lifeboat

Chris groaned. "Could have used that water," he muttered.

Something else fell from the hatch. It turned the ocean around them bright pink. A dye bomb, Josh thought. The pilot was keeping track of them.

The plane rose into the air and flew off, growing smaller and smaller until it disappeared into the distance.

"They came," Josh said. "They'll be back." He heard other

planes, pictured them soaring through the skies. "Look. Spotlights out there!"

Miles away, a spotlight bounced off the clouds. Other beams scanned the ocean. His heart leaped. A search-and-rescue mission was going on over there. Men were being saved. But the raft was drifting. The pink dye began to disappear. Would the pilot find them again?

All night Josh watched distant searchlights scanning the ocean. His arm ached and throbbed. He and Lee pressed their foreheads together, praying.

"Raft's sinking," Chris said.

Josh looked uneasily into the water. The waterlogged life vests that formed a major part of the makeshift raft were sinking. One of the barrels had cracked. Soon, they'd be left swimming. He pictured rows of sharp, jagged teeth.

"Look, over there!" Lee pointed. "A ship!"

All Josh saw were endless rolling swells. Then he spotted it, the lights of a large vessel towering in the foggy night. They had to get its attention. But how? They had no flares. And every moment, the waves were carrying the raft further from the searchlights.

At least some guys were being saved. But the survivors were spread over miles of ocean. Please God, he prayed. Please don't let anyone be left behind. Please let them see us.

He eyed the others' sunburned, blistered faces, their split lips. Alongside him, Lee cradled his burned arm.

Josh gave him a thumbs-up sign.

Be strong, he told himself. Stay strong. It would be worse, much worse to die with rescue so close. But rescue wasn't guaranteed. He knew that now.

CHAPTER 20

FRIDAY AUGUST 4, 1945
THE PHILIPPINE SEA
DAY FIVE | DAWN

AS THE DAWN sky grew pink and gold, Josh jerked awake to the roar of an engine. Again lights flooded the ocean. A seaplane. This time it was coming down.

Wild with excitement, Josh spotted the pilot in the bubble cockpit. *Yes!*

The seaplane banked and circled. The swells were huge. Could it really land in this? Its pontoons hit hard, rose back up into the air, and plowed into the rough water nearby. What an amazing sight. It bobbed in the ocean, around half a mile away.

The men on the raft shouted and waved.

"We're drifting away!" Chris yelled.

Josh groaned, grabbed the broken paddle and began to stroke with the last of his strength.

The seaplane began to taxi slowly. In the other direction. What the heck? Maybe the pilot hadn't even seen them!

Chris let out a frustrated scream. "I'm swimming for it!"

"No way!" Lee caught his life vest.

"I can do it."

"No! Look at the sharks!"

"How do we know the pilot's even seen us?" Chris said. "And we're drifting fast. We can't blow this. It's our one chance."

Tense, eyes glued to their only hope, Josh paddled while Chris, Paul, and Lee screamed and waved life vests.

The seaplane turned. Taxied closer. The side hatch opened and an airman appeared. Josh could see him clearly, a hefty guy with big muscles. He looked like a professional wrestler.

As the seaplane taxied closer, the airman's gaze fastened onto Lee. Not *again*.

The airman's voice rang out. "Hey, sailor! What city do the Dodgers play in?"

What the heck! What was going on now?

"Brooklyn," Josh and Lee shouted in unison.

"Right answer. Sorry! We just had to make sure you guys are Americans!"

Josh closed his eyes. They were shipwrecked in shark territory and he had to answer questions about the Dodgers. Lucky he got it right. Lucky his mind hadn't gone totally whacko.

"I'm Morgan Hensley," the hefty guy shouted, "Hang on. We're going to get you outta here!"

A rope ladder dropped down and the airman climbed onto the rungs. They were safe. They really were safe. Josh breathed a prayer of thanks.

"Steady! Got a few injured ones here, sir," someone said.

"Get them onto the plane. That float looks ready to sink."

Strong hands pulled Josh out of the raft. With a burst of strength, he grabbed the rope ladder.

Suddenly, the hefty airman shouted in alarm. "Sharks! Look at the sharks! Layers of them!"

"Omigod, they're everywhere!" another airman shouted. "Look at the size of them!"

"Yeah. I know." Josh didn't look. He didn't need to see sharks. He'd seen enough. He didn't want to see more. Ever.

Whipped by wind and spray, the ladder swung and swayed. Josh white-knuckled each rung as he hauled himself up with his good hand. Rifle shots rang out. The men on the plane were firing at the sharks. Way to go.

Almost leaping through the seaplane door, he flopped onto the floor and lay there, giving the pilot a big grin. He was safe.

Lee, Chris, and Paul were hauled on board, followed soon by other stunned-looking men. Survivors laughed, cried, shouted, and vomited.

"I can't believe you came!" a sailor shouted, tears streaming down his face.

"I can't believe you took so long!" someone growled.

Soon the fuselage of the plane was packed totally full of men. Still more survivors were tied to the plane wings with parachute cord.

The pilot, a young man with kind, fierce eyes, surveyed the survivors, frowning at the oil-covered bodies, festering wounds, and sunken cheeks.

"I'm Adrian Marks," he said. "You're safe now, sailors. Just take it easy. We're trying to get as many of you as we can, and the ships will get the rest."

Lieutenant Marks and the plane's crew bathed and bandaged the survivors' wounds as they taxied up and down the towering waves, searching for more survivors.

Morgan, the hefty crewman, sat next to Josh and fed him spoonfuls of sugar water. "We saw your heads down there," Morgan said. "Couldn't see much though, because of all the oil. You guys are like pickled in oil, yeah?"

Josh said, "Why didn't you come days ago?"

Lieutenant Marks said, "No one even knew the USS Indianapolis was in trouble. Thank God we saw you."

"But the radio operator sent an SOS," Josh said. "I saw him go down there."

"Well, no one had a clue you were missing," Morgan said. "When we spotted you, we didn't even know if you guys were American or Japanese. And then we saw the sharks." He grimaced. "When the Lieutenant saw that, he decided to help no matter who you were. The Navy said the seas were too rough to land. But we did it anyway." He grinned. "The Navy refused Lieutenant Marks permission to touch down. But he disobeyed orders. Messed up the plane's pontoons, though."

"I'm sure glad you did," Josh said. "Real glad!"

Suddenly he noticed the floor was wet. And getting wetter. He slid his good hand over it. Pulled himself up fast. "Plane's sprung a leak, Sir."

Josh, Lee, Morgan and three other able-bodied survivors began bailing furiously. Josh's injured arm throbbed with pain but he had priorities. He was not going down into that ocean again. No way.

"That should do it! We're taking off," the pilot called.

"Well done, sailor," Morgan said.

Josh grinned. Wish I could tell Dad about all of this, he thought. Wish I could tell him about Lee and Morgan and the pilot. He'd have liked these guys. Wish I could tell him how I got away from those sharks.

He lay back and took a deep, deep breath of relief. "Home," he said. "We're really going home."

"You gonna visit me in Hawaii?" Lee said.

"You bet," Josh replied. "If you let me drive that sports car around the island."

"Sounds good."

Too exhausted to talk, they lay back as the seaplane flew low over the ocean toward the hospital ship.

I'm safe! Josh thought. No more sharks! I'm going home.

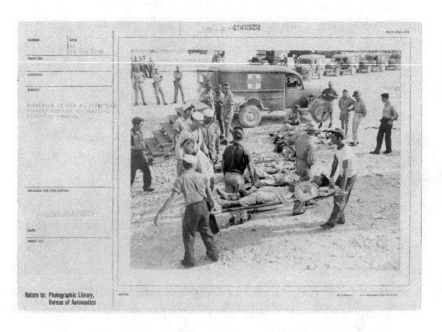

USS Indianapolis survivors enroute to hospital following their rescue.

CHAPTER 21

JOSH WAS GOING DOWN, down. Into the pitch-black. The shark was after him. Coming at him. Right at him.

Josh shouted. Kicked. Hit out furiously. *Not now! Not again!*

"Hey! Hey, Josh, wake up! It's over, man. We're safe."

Josh lurched upright in the narrow hospital cot. In the next one over, Lee's sunburned face had finally stopped peeling and his infection was nearly gone. Pete, his red hair a sleep-wild frizz, was on his feet.

"Sorry," Josh groaned.

"No problem," Pete said. Josh noticed a tall, uniformed officer at his friend's side. "I want you to meet my cousin. Lieutenant Mike Bennet."

Josh jumped out of bed, trying to straighten his rumpled T-shirt and shorts. His injured arm was still heavily bandaged. He stuck out his good one. "Pleased to meet you, sir."

Mike smiled warmly, shaking hands with Josh and Lee. He gave Pete a bear hug. "How are you all feeling?"

Josh rubbed his swollen limb. He could feel the punctures where the shark had sunk its teeth. He gave an embarrassed grin. "Guess I was yelling in my sleep. Just wrestling sharks."

"I had a mind-blowing nightmare last night," Pete said. "Dreamed I was swimming for that make-believe island, with the sharks coming after me. Guess we'll all have nightmares for a while."

"A heck of a lot's been happening since I waved goodbye to you at the harbor in San Francisco," Mike said.

The three boys listened warily. The scraps of news they'd received about the escalating war had grown worse day by day. Already, millions had died. And millions more were expected to die, fighting the Japanese in the Pacific in the coming months.

Mike's tense expression mirrored theirs. "I guess you heard the Japanese warlords refused to surrender."

"Yeah," Josh said. "We were hoping the Japanese emperor would convince them to back down."

"Nope," Mike said. "Not even the Soviet Union declaring war on their country has stopped them. President Truman has vowed to destroy Japan's power to attack the United States again. He won't let them strike Los Angeles or San Francisco the way they slaughtered our people at Pearl Harbor."

Mike was quiet for a moment. What he said next was more unbelievable than anything Josh had ever heard.

"Day before yesterday, we dropped a bomb on Japan's military base at Hiroshima. Another bomb was dropped on Nagasaki today." Mike's face was grim. "The president's about to make a news broadcast." He put his hand on Pete's shoulder. "I wanted to be with you guys."

Josh felt his body tense. Was the war growing even worse? He glanced at Lee. His friend had tears in his eyes.

"This is all terrible," Josh said. He didn't know what else to say.

Lee grimaced, "War is a terrible thing."

The quietness of the hospital ward was shattered as men gathered around the radio, talking animatedly to one another, trying to guess what the news broadcast would be about.

"As soon as they let me out of here," one said, "I'll be fighting again. We'll stop Japan. We have to."

"Yeah," someone said. "I don't want them coming after my family."

"They killed nine hundred of our mates on the Indy," someone else said.

Mike nodded. "And thousands upon thousands more across the globe. Our best and bravest."

"This has to stop."

The radio had been playing soft ragtime music. Now the music came to an abrupt halt. Someone turned it up. For a few moments, it hummed with loud static. Then a voice came over the airwaves.

Pete whirled around, silencing the survivors in the ward. "Listen! It's the press conference. It's President Truman!"

When Josh heard President Truman's deep voice, his heart sped up. He hoped some awful new thing hadn't happened.

"This is the day we have been waiting for since Pearl Harbor," President Truman said. "This is the day when Fascism finally dies, as we always knew it would."

What did that mean? Was the war over? How?

Around him, gaunt faces brightened and eyes widened with shock and joy. The war was over!

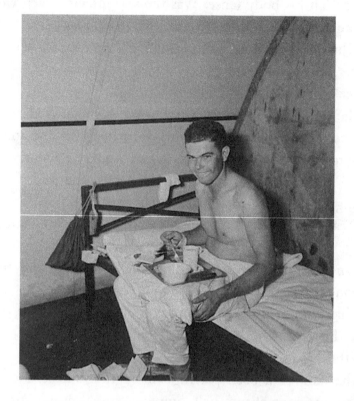

Actual USS Indianapolis Survivor Curtis Pace, S2c USNR

The Indy sailors who'd been lucky enough to survive the gruesome torpedo attack listened in silence.

President Truman informed the nation that the Japanese Emperor Hirohito had surrendered to the Allied Forces. The United States had brought an end to the War in the Pacific. It had brought an end to World War II.

"Arrangements are now being made for the signing of the surrender terms at the earliest possible moment," President Truman said.

Wow! Just like that! After six long, terrible years, World War II was finally over. Josh couldn't believe his ears. *The war is over!*

The hospital ward erupted in ear-shattering cheers and clapping. From the radio, Josh heard the sound of loud cheering, too. Survivors hugged one another. Some broke down and sobbed with relief. Even the badly injured raised their arms high in victory. Relief flooded Josh. Relief and joy. The Japanese had surrendered! World War II was finally over! It felt as if a huge weight had lifted from his chest.

Mike grinned and shouted for attention. "There's more. I came to tell you something," he said. "You men played a big part in bringing an end to this war. Remember the crate and canister the Marines loaded aboard in San Francisco?"

"Yeah," Josh nodded. He recalled the sinister, big steel canister in particular. And the heavily armed Marines that had guarded it.

"That crate contained the parts for the atomic bomb," Mike said. "The canister contained the radioactive plutonium."

Josh gaped. On that awful night when the torpedo struck, Pete had told him the USS Indianapolis was on a secret mission. So that was the mission. "The bomb was in the crates we had on the Indy? The crates we offloaded on Tinian Island?"

"Yeah. That bomb is what finally convinced Japan to surrender. The bomb ended the war."

"Wow."

The survivors of the USS Indianapolis shook their heads in amazement and began to talk loudly.

Josh was flooded with relief, but also something he couldn't quite understand. He was glad they'd won. Glad his dad's death had been avenged. But Lee's words stuck with him. War was a terrible thing.

"I think you'll all be up for Purple Hearts," Mike said. "The aircrew who dropped the bomb heard how you guys suffered, how your shipmates died out there in the ocean. Before they dropped the bomb, someone wrote on it in black marker across its side: *This one is for the boys of the USS Indianapolis.*"

Josh sank back down on his bed. Double wow! He longed to tell his dad.

He pictured arriving back home. Mom running to greet him, hugging him as hard as she could. Telling him she was furious with him for leaving, for joining the Navy. Then whispering she was proud of him. He pictured hugging his little brother. Showing Sammy his shark bite wounds. Teaching Sammy how to pitch a ball. Thanksgiving's coming soon, he thought. *I can't wait to eat pumpkin pie!*

Thoughts whirled around in his head. World War II was over! It seemed it would never end. For what seemed an eternity, he thought he'd die in the ocean. Be eaten by sharks. Never come back at all.

But the war ended. He escaped the sharks. He was going home.

I'll do the best I can, he thought. I'll be there for Mom and Sammy, like Dad asked me to be. I'll try and fill in for him. He sighed. I wish Dad was here. I wish I could talk to him.

And then he realized that his dad was right there. In his head. In his heart. He'd heard his familiar, strong voice so many times as he'd struggled to stay alive. He could almost hear it now: *Hang in there, son. Don't quit.*

"*I did it, Dad,*" he whispered. "*I did it. I hung in there. I didn't quit. I'm going home. I escaped.*"

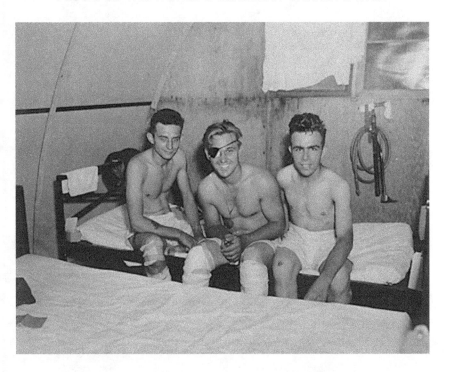

Actual USS Indianapolis survivors: (L to R) Michael N.
Kuryla, Jr., Cox. USNR; Robert M. McGwiggam, S1c USNR;
and John H. Armistead, S2c, USNR

Eight hundred and seventy nine men lost their lives during those terrible five days.

Three hundred and sixteen men survived despite dire circumstances.

We salute and remember the brave sailors of the USS Indianapolis.

SURVIVOR QUOTES

"Every few minutes you'd see their fins - a dozen to two dozen fins in the water. They would come up and bump you. I was bumped a few times - you never know when they are going to attack you." - *Loel Dean Cox, Seaman Second Class*

"you could see the sharks eating your comrade." - *Granville Crane, Machinist's Mate Second Class*

"I didn't even have a life jacket, so I was swimming from midnight to 5:30 in the morning." - *Lyle Umenhoffer, Seaman First Class*

"It's much easier to die than it is to live. You've got to struggle to live." - *Edgar Harrell, Marine Corporal*

"When I was in the water and I wanted to give up, I saw my dad's face, and I wasn't going to give up for him. He brought me home." - *Dick Thelen, Seaman Second Class*

FAST FACTS ABOUT THE DISASTER

- The Indy sank on July 30, 1945, near the end of World War II
- It was struck by a Japanese torpedo
- It sank in only 12 minutes
- The survivors lacked the most basic survival gear. Many were without life jackets.
- They were rescued by chance when a PV-1 Ventura spotted them on routine patrol
- Total crewmen aboard: 1,195
- Total crewmen who went down with the ship: Approx. 300
- Initial survivor count in the ocean after sinking: Approx. 900
- Only 316 men survived

DID YOU KNOW?

The sinking of the USS Indianapolis resulted in the largest number of shark attacks on humans in history.

WHAT DREW SO MANY SHARKS?

Receptors on sharks' bodies pick up pressure changes and movement in the ocean. They can smell blood and urine from hundreds of yards away. With nine hundred men bobbing up and down in the waves—many injured and bleeding—sharks were naturally attracted to the area. Each day brought more sharks, all drawn by the survivors' blood and movements, as well as the scent of the dead.

WORLD'S DEADLIEST NAVAL DISASTER

The sinking of the USS Indianapolis also led to the greatest single loss of life at sea, from a single ship, in the history of the US Navy. The warship had just finished a trip to United States Army Air Force Base at Tinian to deliver parts of Little Boy, the first nuclear weapon ever used in combat, and was on her way to the Philippines to prepare for the invasion of Japan.

WHY DID NO ONE COME?

Questions remain today about why the rescue was delayed for so long. Originally, the Navy claimed no distress signal had been sent. However, the survivors knew SOS messages had gone out. In fact, *other ships reported receiving the distress signals!*

Here are two possible reasons:

1. The Navy might have thought the signals were fake because when Navy officials tried to contact the ship, they got no reply. Of course, the Indy couldn't reply. The warship had already gone down.

2. When Navy intelligence officials captured a Japanese submarine's signals claiming that it sank a warship along the Indy's route, they thought it was a hoax. Tragically, they believed the Japanese were trying to convince American rescue ships to come there so they could ambush and destroy them.

MORE COMMUNICATION PROBLEMS

At the time, only non-fighting ships (ones carrying supplies and services) had to report their arrival to the Navy. Leyte Gulf had more than 1,500 ships reporting in preparation for the expected Japanese invasion.

The USS Indianapolis, however, was a fighting ship. A warship. So when it didn't show up on schedule, no one cared. It was none of their business. The ship was not required to check in.

TOP SECRET FAIL?

Some historians argue that communications between the USS Indianapolis and the Navy were minimized because the warship was on such a secret mission, carrying the atomic bomb.

MOVIES AND REPELLENTS

The horrific tales of shark attacks spurred new military research into shark repellents.

The tragic event inspired film makers and writers to tell the survivors' stories. There are numerous fiction and non-fiction accounts of the voyage, plus a 2007 television documentary film *Ocean of Fear: Worst Shark Attack Ever.* The movie, *USS Indianapolis, Men of Courage,* starring Nicolas Cage, premiered in 2016.

In a scene from the blockbuster movie *Jaws,* the character Quaint (Robert Shaw) recounts his experience surviving the sinking of the Indianapolis. Quint's harrowing story presents a true depiction of this strange and tragic event.

- Sharks are the apex predators of the ocean.
- Sharks have strong jaws, but they're not the strongest in the animal kingdom. Instead, they rely on slicing and head-shaking to rip off chunks of flesh
- Sharks have multiple rows of teeth. Some have two or three rows, some as many as fifteen.
- Sharks have excellent vision. Their night vision is better than that of cats or wolves.
- A shark's sense of smell is 10,000 times better than a human's. Sharks can smell a drop of blood in the water.
- Sharks have incredible hearing and can hear movement in the water from miles away.
- Sharks can detect electrical impulses, such as a human's beating heart.
- Unlike humans, whose jaws are fixed and can only open so wide, sharks can *unhinge* their jaws to grab and hang on to prey.
- Oceanic whitetip sharks are found in the deep open ocean. The species is known for feeding frenzies.
- Oceanic whitetip shark numbers are declining because they're the main ingredient in shark fin soup.
- The biggest shark is the whale shark. It can grow to over 66 in length.
- The fastest shark is the mako shark. It can reach speeds of 60 miles per hour when hunting.
- Sharks must keep moving or they'll drown.

- The odds of being attacked by a shark are low. More people are killed by cows and dogs. Most shark species generally do not attack humans.
- The most aggressive shark species are: the great white shark, the striped tiger shark and the bull shark.

LOWER YOUR CHANCES OF GETTING BIT

- Always swim in a group. Sharks usually attack lone individuals.
- Stay close to shore.
- Avoid the water at night, dawn, or dusk when sharks are more active, and better able to see you than you are to see them.
- Keep away from river mouths, particularly after it rains.
- Never enter the water if injured, bleeding, or menstruating. Sharks can smell and taste blood and track it from a long way away.
- Avoid wearing shiny jewelry. The reflected light looks like shining fish scales.
- Don't swim where sewage could be present. Sewage attracts bait fish and sharks.
- Stay away from fishing boats and anywhere people are fishing—particularly with bait.
- Leave immediately if a shark is seen.
- Avoid brightly colored clothes. Orange and yellow are said to attract sharks, as do contrasting colors.
- Avoid cloudy waters.
- Don't splash a lot or make seal noises.
- Keep pets out of the water.

- Avoid sandbars or steep drop-offs where sharks hang out.
- Remember that porpoises, seabirds, and turtles often eat the same foods as sharks. If turtles or fish behave erratically, leave the water.
- Don't touch a shark.
- If diving and approached by a shark, stay as still as possible. If you are carrying fish, release the fish.
- Report shark sightings to authorities

WHAT TO DO IF A SHARK ATTACKS

Do whatever you can to get away. Don't use your bare hands or feet if you can avoid it, as the shark's skin can scrape you.

If necessary, aim at the shark's delicate eyes, gills, or snout. Pound the shark in every way possible. Claw or jab at the eyes and gill openings. Shout for help.

Do not play dead.

If bitten, try to leave the water calmly and swiftly. While many sharks will not bite again, you cannot rule out a second attack.

Try to stop the bleeding. If surfing or bodyboarding, use the leash as a tourniquet.

Get immediate medical attention.

HOW TO HELP A SHARK BITE VICTIM

- Control the bleeding by applying firm pressure, by tightly wrapping the injury, or with a tourniquet.
- Remove the person from the water as soon as possible

- Protect victim from cold by wrapping in blanket or towels to minimize heat loss.
- Do not move victim unnecessarily.
- Call 911 for immediate medical help.

A FINAL NOTE

Sharks are dangerous but we must remember that the ocean is their home. They play an important role in keeping the oceans in balance. The United States is a leader in promoting the global conservation and management of sharks. To learn more, visit:

https://www.fisheries.noaa.gov/national/international-affairs/shark-conservation

---

USS INDIANAPOLIS • FURTHER READING
Left for Dead by Pete Nelson
In Harm's Way by Doug Stanton
Fatal Voyage by Dan Kurzman

STUDY GUIDE
Download this book's
reading comprehension guides at
http://bit.ly/sharkescape

How Hunter Scott, a 12-year-old boy cleared Captain McVay's Name

Charles Butler McVay was the USS Indianapolis's commanding officer when she was torpedoed and lost in action in 1945. He survived, only to be court-martialed by the US Navy and found guilty for the disaster!

This angered many survivors. They believed McVay was not at fault.

Instead, many believed the US Navy was using McVay as a scapegoat to cover up their own messy mistake. After all, the Navy *didn't even go searching* for the survivors! Over eleven-hundred men were left to die at sea. The last three hundred still alive were saved only because of a chance flyover. How could McVay be responsible for that?

Hunter Scott, a 12-year-old Pensacola, Florida student wrote about the USS Indianapolis for a National History Day project. During his research, Hunter formed the conclusion that the Navy had unjustly convicted Captain McVay. Although decades had passed and Captain McVay was no longer alive, Hunter wanted to act. He was horrified by the shameful court-martial of an innocent man who'd fought for this country. Hunter decided to raise awareness about this miscarriage of justice and try to overturn McVay's sentence.

Hunter's project won first prize at his school and first place at the county-finals. In the 1997 state finals, however, his project was disqualified. Why? His display of three-ring notebooks was ruled an infraction!

Hunter felt bad. He'd failed to repair Captain McVay's legacy and had disappointed the survivors who were counting on him. *Never give up*, the sailors, now in their seventies, said. Hunter was sure they knew all about never giving up! He decided to keep fighting. But he was just a twelve-year-old kid trying to reverse a fifty-year-old injustice.

Luckily, Pensacola is a Navy city. Hunter's determined efforts attracted media attention. Pensacola newspapers ran articles about Hunter, then TV station NBC took up the story.

This is a middle school history project that seeks to correct history, said the newspapers and TV anchors.

At a USS Indianapolis reunion, the survivors welcomed Hunter. Adrian Marks, the pilot who'd risked his lift to land in twelve-foot waves and pluck out the wounded was there. When Hunter told them that he'd interviewed nearly one hundred and fifty Indy survivors and had reviewed eight hundred documents, the men were stunned.

Kimo McVay, Captain McVay's son, had been trying to clear his dad's name for over fifty years. He said Hunter had gotten further with his research than he and the survivors had in half a century!

Excited, Hunter, Kimo McVay, and a group of survivors banded together and headed for Washington DC to lobby Congress. They hoped somebody could overturn or reverse the guilty verdict. To do so, they'd have to move a bill through Congress, a difficult and time-consuming operation.

With the support of his Congressman, Hunter appeared before the US Congress, alongside the USS Indianapolis survivors. Hunter explained to the senators why McVay should be exonerated. The government was unaware of many facts he'd uncovered in his research.

Here's one example: the Navy received the Indy's desperate SOS signals—but Navy officials believed the SOS signals were a Japanese hoax. That's why they didn't respond! They didn't even bother to check to see if the ship was missing.

After years of efforts to clear Captain McVay's name, the survivors, Kimo McVay, and Hunter Scott finally succeeded. In October 2000, the United States Congress passed a resolution that McVay's record should reflect that "he is exonerated for the loss of the USS Indianapolis." President Clinton also signed the resolution.

In July 2001, Secretary of the Navy Gordon R. England ordered McVay's official Navy record purged of all wrongdoing.

Hunter went on to study economics and physics at the University of North Carolina at Chapel Hill on a Naval ROTC scholarship. In 2017, Lieutenant Hunter Scott, USN, became a Naval Aviator on the flight deck of USS Bonhomme Richard. He has shown what one determined child can do by never giving up.

THE I ESCAPED BOOKS

I Escaped North Korea!

I Escaped The California Camp Fire

I Escaped The World's Deadliest Shark Attack

coming soon

I Escaped Amazon Jungle Pirates

MORE BOOKS BY ELLIE CROWE

Kamehameha: The Boy Who Became a Warrior King

Nelson Mandela—The Boy Called Troublemaker

Surfer of the Century: The Life of Duke Kahanamoku

Wind Runner

MORE BOOKS BY SCOTT PETERS

Mystery of the Egyptian Scroll

Mystery of the Egyptian Amulet

Mystery of the Egyptian Temple

Mystery of the Egyptian Mummy

Join the *I Escaped Club* to hear about new releases at:

https://tinyurl.com/escaped-club